Winning Streak

Katie Kenyhercz

Wishing you love, hugs
and hockey!

Katie

CRIMSON
ROMANCE

F+W Media, Inc.

Published by
Crimson Romance
an imprint of F+W Media, Inc.
10151 Carver Road, Suite 200
Blue Ash, OH 45242. U.S.A.
www.crimsonromance.com

ISBN 10: 1-4405-8408-7
ISBN 13: 978-1-4405-8408-4
eISBN 10: 1-4405-8409-5
eISBN 13: 978-1-4405-8409-1

This is a work of fiction. Names, characters, corporations, institutions, organizations, events, or locales in this novel are either the product of the author's imagination or, if real, used fictitiously. The resemblance of any character to actual persons (living or dead) is entirely coincidental.

Cover art ©123RF/Konstantin Sutyagin and iStock/Yuri

This one is for my brothers, Mike and Will. Their love and loyalty inspired the best parts of Madden. I couldn't ask for better friends or protectors. They are all-around amazing, and I am so proud to be their sister. I love you both!

Chapter One

Wednesday, February 19th

Few things were manlier than eating with your hands and watching guys fight gladiator-style in suits of armor. It was the perfect way to kick off a friend's bachelor party and almost good enough to distract Madden Vaughn from the fact that his ex was getting married shortly in Excalibur's chapel. Yep, his brother-in-law, Carter, decided Shane Reese's bachelor party should have a medieval theme. On the same day as Linden's wedding. As a part of the Las Vegas Sinners brotherhood—albeit in management and not on the team—not to mention a groomsman, Madden couldn't exactly beg off.

Was there something in the air? Everyone he knew was settling down, but the thought made his skin itch. Thanks to Linden's particular brand of manipulation, the single life suited him just fine. Okay, not every woman would use him as a pawn to get at his sister because she owned the Sinners hockey team, but in this case it was once burned, ten times shy. So why did he even care if the evil reporter was getting married?

People around him cheered as the good knights defeated Mordred, the fire wizard, and Madden licked the gravy off his fingers before clapping along. The arena lights came up as the smoke cleared, and the crowd started filing out.

"All right, boys. Let's go to Octane and really get this party started." Carter slapped Reese, the groom-to-be, on the back and led their group out of the arena. Madden brought up the rear alongside his best friend and roommate, Sinners captain Dylan Cole.

Newly twenty-two, the kid was hardly typical for his age. While his teammates were loud and rowdy, Cole was quiet and a little shy, which made him a great secret-keeper. He lowered his voice as the others walked ahead. "So, how you hangin' in?"

Madden shrugged. "I'm trying to focus on the positives. We just ate Cornish hens with our hands, are about to indulge in some top-shelf alcohol at a motorcycle-themed bar, and we're celebrating our friend."

"You held up pretty well in the casino. Proud of ya."

That part hadn't been easy. The others wanted to take in some craps games before the tournament, which was fine for them. They weren't recovering gambling addicts. Had his brother-in-law gotten there earlier, he might have tried to talk them out of it, being the only one who understood how deep Madden had gotten into that world, but Carter got stuck in traffic and Madden didn't want to hold the group back.

He'd white-knuckled it as casually as he could for a half hour and walked out of the room of flashing lights and rolling dice unscathed. Kevin Scott won big and divvied up his chips with everyone. Accepting a few might not have been the best idea. They'd burned a hole in Madden's jacket pocket through the entire medieval experience. But he didn't have to go back to that casino, and he wouldn't. No way was he tossing aside the last two years of not placing a single bet.

On the way into the bar, a few guys huddled around a pristine motorcycle in a glass case under the glowing Octane sign. Madden went straight to the counter and winked at the sexy bartender in a leather bustier. "Hey, beautiful. How about a Corona?"

Cole stepped up beside him. "Make it two."

The woman smiled at Madden, then gave Cole a once-over. "Can I see your ID, sweetie?"

Poor kid. He'd get carded into his forties. Women might enjoy that, but for a man, it was embarrassing. It didn't seem to faze Cole though. They took their beers, and Madden tipped the tender a twenty.

"Hold on there, stud." She wrote her number on a napkin and tucked it in his hand. "Call me sometime."

"My pleasure."

They sat at a steel-topped table, and Cole leaned forward. "How do you *do* that? I mean, I'm happy with Tricia. I'm just curious. Flirting is like your super power."

"What can I say? Women find me irresistible." Except the one getting married right around the corner. He took a long pull from the Corona. He was no longer the hard partier he'd once been, but tonight called for a little liquid anesthetic. The other guys joined them, and for the next hour, he let the good times flow.

It was on the fourth round of drinks that he pushed back his chair. "Sorry to be the first to go, but it's time for me to head home." The group groaned and taunted, but he waved them off.

"I'm with Madden. And the rest of you should think about it. We *do* have practice tomorrow." Cole pulled a tip out of his wallet and threw it on the table.

The men smirked, but that observation had merit. Their coach was a tiny terror who would castrate them if they couldn't skate.

Reese raised his glass. "A man gets married once in a lifetime if he's lucky. I don't mind taking some flak from Coach."

The others lifted their glasses in agreement. Cole shook his head. "Your funerals. Later."

Madden led the way through the crowd but halted outside of Octane and rocked back on his heels, closing his eyes to stop the hall from tilting.

"You okay?"

He checked his watch. "Yeah. Fine. Mind if we walk the food court for a minute? Think I need to grab a coffee."

"Sure. No problem."

That wasn't the best idea. The food court was full of strong, greasy, spicy scents, and after one lap, they ducked into Starbucks. At least the smell of freshly brewed Colombian beans didn't turn his stomach upside down. They got two cups to go and sipped the buzz-clearing brew on the way out.

The wedding should be over now.

But what if it wasn't? The coffee soured in his stomach, and the back of his neck felt hot and cold at the same time. They had to walk by the chapel to get to the elevators. It was hard enough passing it on the way in, but it had been empty then. As they got closer, the officiant's voice came through the doors. "Repeat after me. I, Linden, take you, Walter ... " *Oh shit.*

He had to see. Just one look to end one of the worst chapters of his life. "Hold this." He handed Cole his coffee and pressed a hand flat to one of the doors.

"Hey, man, I don't think this is a good—"

Madden held a hand up to cut him off and eased the door open a crack. Only one side of pews fit into his line of vision, so he leaned a little more. The aisle came into view, and at the top of it, Linden repeated the officiant's words and slid a ring onto *Walter's* finger. What kind of name was that anyway?

Cole tried to lean around him, and the door swung wide. Madden fell onto the red carpet runner, and every head in the place swiveled in his direction. He jumped to his feet and brushed himself off. "Uh, sorry, folks." Linden stared at him with open shock that quickly turned to anger. He about-faced and pushed through the doors to find Cole holding the elevator open.

Madden's pulse didn't slow until they were on the ground floor.

"You still staying positive?" Cole asked.

"I'm positive I need another drink."

Chapter Two

"Dude, you don't look so hot."

Madden opened one eye to find Cole squatting by the couch that had served as his bed for the night and might serve as his final resting place if the blinding headache were any indicator. Well, the outline of Cole. His hangover and the gray, pre-dawn light coming through the thin curtains made details fuzzy.

"Thanks for the breaking news. Aren't you late for practice?"

"Almost. That was some night you had. Just wanted to make sure you were alive."

"Jury's still out. But *you* won't be alive if Neals sees you stroll in one minute past seven." Nealy Windham, head coach of the Sinners, would deafen the poor kid and anyone else within a ten-mile radius of her sonic screech if his blades weren't on the ice as soon as she blew the whistle. Goading Cole out the door was a public service. And, okay, a personal one, if it meant Madden could have fifteen minutes of blessed silence before showering for work himself.

"I'm gone. Catch you later."

Madden closed his eyes to the rustle of a duffle bag and the torturous banging of the front door. Outside, an engine started then faded away, and his muscles went slack. *That was some night you had.* Yeah, no kidding. The image of Linden's shocked face almost made him laugh, but the vision of her in that fitted, white, medieval dress squashed it.

He swung his legs over the side of the couch and leveraged himself to a sitting position. Ugh—not easy to count that as a victory when it unleashed a torrent of stabbing needles in his skull. He pushed to his feet and swallowed back the nausea, feeling his way to the kitchen. Nearly three years in the cavernous mansion his father had left him, and he'd finally learned the place well enough to navigate with his eyes closed. Not that drunken stumbling was something he did often anymore.

A couple painkillers and a quick, cold shower didn't change how he looked or felt, but he was conscious at least. On his way to work, he swung by McDonald's for black coffee and hash browns, the staples of any good hangover helper kit. He sat in the underground garage of the Las Vegas Arena and let the greasy food and liquid energy do its work while he prepared to deal with his sister.

Their father had left the Sinners to Jacey—honestly, a smart move on his part—and she ran the team with a manicured, platinum fist. As assistant GM, he had responsibilities, but only one that had potential to damage the team: Keep a clean public image. She'd repeated it so many times, she'd threatened a forehead tattoo as the next step. And he'd been good. For two years. But sometimes the universe conspired to obliterate your best intentions. It might have had some help from a few beers. And unlike the tourists, what happened to *him* in Vegas got reported directly to his sister.

Feeling a little more human, or at least a solid seventy percent sure he wouldn't lose his gourmet breakfast, he key-fobbed into the building. Down the hall, muted whistles, shouts, and frantic skates echoed from the other side of the locker room. Thank God for the silent and dim elevator. It opened at the executive level with a new rush of light and sound that made the room spin for a second. He blinked hard then made for his office, head down. He reached for the knob, but Jacey's hand caught his and held on.

"Not so fast, Maddie."

He glanced around, but no one seemed to have heard the embarrassing nickname. "Not in public, remember?"

"Funny. I think I said the same thing to you about being an ass. And yet … "

"I swear. Last night wasn't my fault—"

"Uh-uh. Save it. I don't have time for a speech today so I'm delegating."

"You're … what?" Sure, their father had chimed in occasionally, but Jacey'd had sole responsibility for lecturing him his entire life. To be fair, he'd given her plenty of opportunities, but that was in the past. Well, until about twelve hours ago.

Then the important part of her statement came back to him. Horror turned his skin clammy as he imagined his brother-in-law and the acting GM having to wring him out to dry. Metaphorically, even though the guy could do serious physical damage as the ex-captain of the team. Madden tried to swallow, but his throat wouldn't cooperate. "Come on, Sis. Carter doesn't have to—"

"Not Carter." Jacey tugged him into the office across the hall, where Saralynn Reese, the new head of Sinners PR, stood behind her desk looking like sex in a suit. With a scowl. *Oh damn.*

• • •

She'd been expecting him, so at least he was the only one with dumb surprise on his chiseled, boy-band face. It lacked its usual luster, the confident glow replaced with sallow pallor. He wore sunglasses, but Saralynn would bet the twinkle in his blue eyes was currently downgraded to a faint twinge.

Jacey pushed him forward and raised a hand as if to say, *He's all yours; good luck.* Then she left the room and closed the door. Madden stood behind the chair opposite the desk and shoved his hands in his pockets. "Look, I don't know what my sister told you, but I—"

"Oh, I didn't hear about it from Jacey." She let that sink in. It took a second, but then his face crumpled, and he palmed his forehead. She smiled. "You were at my *brother's* bachelor party. You think we don't talk? I got drunk dialed last night." Her brother, the team goalie, had actually met his match, and the wedding was on Saturday. As if she didn't have enough to do getting ready for *that,* now she got to deal with Madden, the PR nightmare. From the day she got the job, she'd known it was only a matter of time, but couldn't he have waited one more week?

He pulled the chair behind him and slumped into it, cradling his head in both hands. Big, pale fingers, pink at the knuckles, dug into strawberry blond spikes, and sympathy pricked at her heart. Even if the giant oaf brought this trouble on himself.

She eased into her own chair and crossed her legs. "I'm missing some details, though, which is what I need from you. Reese only remembered the highlights." Some thought it strange she called her brother by their last name, but goalies were strange, and everyone here knew that. Skipping the explanations was one of the many perks of this job.

Madden raised his head slowly and took off the shades. How 'bout that? Even bloodshot, those gray-blue eyes managed to twinkle. "You mean I'm not here to get my ass handed to me?"

She bit the inside of her cheek to fight a grin at the image of his ass. She'd seen it around the arena now and then, and a fine one it was. Unfortunately, it wasn't the topic of their first actual conversation. "What am I, your guardian? My job is damage control. This isn't the principal's office."

A frown accentuated his full lower lip. "Then I don't understand. Last night was one of my worst personally, but I don't see what that has to do with the—"

She dropped the day's issue of *The Las Vegas Sun* on her desk, specifically the local section. His eyes widened as he stared at a picture of himself on hands and knees just inside the chapel doors and the headline above the fold. *Sinners' assistant GM crashes ex's wedding,* by Linden East.

"Jesus. The photographer wasn't aimed at me. I remember that."

"Came from a cell phone. I'm guessing on the bride's side. I need you to help me downgrade this from a tornado to a thunderstorm."

He sighed. "Yeah. All right. What do you need?"

"Reese says you were with the group most of the night. You'd seen the jousting show and drank yourselves stupid at Octane. Things were winding down, and guys started to beg off. He says he didn't actually see you leave the building."

"I didn't leave, and I was only half drunk. The other half came later."

"So you half-soberly decided to crash your ex's Knights of the Round Table wedding."

He squeezed his eyes shut for a long second. "You have any aspirin? I took a couple this morning, but I don't think it was enough."

She held her tongue, dug a bottle out of her top drawer, and slid it to him.

He downed two and slid it back. "Thanks. I don't know what I was thinking. I guess not anything. I saw the announcement in the paper last week and tried to forget it. But then Reese's bachelor party was in the same building." He gave a quick recount of the rest of the night, ending with, "Cole held my coffee while I made an ass of myself."

Thank God for small favors. If Cole's face had been in the paper, too, her job would be double hard.

"So … Jace is pretty pissed, huh? She probably thinks I'm an idiot for going anywhere near Linden again."

That twinge of sympathy in her chest got a little bigger. Madden, the one person on earth who was a bigger flirt than even she used to be, seemed to genuinely care about Linden, the bitter reporter who not too long ago put him and the whole team through a media circus. "Sisters understand brothers being stupid about girls. Trust me. If she's pissed, it's probably because Linden insinuated you were gambling last night. She said when you crashed in, some chips fell out of your pocket."

Saralynn might as well have slapped him. Shock clouded his face, and he reached a new shade of pale just before the hurt took over. It was there and gone in seconds as he shut down. "I didn't gamble. Do you need anything else?"

An explanation would be good, but he clearly was no longer in a mood to cooperate. She lifted her chin. "I'll let you know."

He pushed out of the chair and left her office. Instead of going to his, he headed back toward the elevator. Saralynn closed her eyes and whispered, "Not my problem. Not my problem." Her list was big enough.

Chapter Three

Alize at the top of the Palms should've seemed huge for a restaurant that could seat 130 and currently held only the nineteen people that made up the Reese bridal party. Instead, it felt microscopic as he sat across from his sister, who looked anywhere but at him. Madden pushed roasted tomato slices and mashed potatoes around the rib eye on his plate. It all looked good, but he couldn't eat. Jacey hadn't answered his call the night before and hadn't looked him in the eye all day.

No one seemed to notice the rift, but that was probably because his sister was a master at hiding her problems. If he hadn't spent his whole life watching her play Supergirl, he might not have noticed either. But he'd also had a lifetime's experience of seeing her disappointed, so the subtle signs were clear. Sure, she'd said a word or two to him when it was necessary, but not otherwise. She took every opportunity to be at least ten feet away, and when he'd tried to talk to her after the ceremony run-through, she'd suddenly had to use the restroom.

It was Reese and Allie's night, and Jacey wouldn't do anything to compromise it. But this felt like more than that. Like she'd be avoiding him for a while. He leaned over his plate and lowered his voice below the background conversation. "Jace … "

She glanced at him from the corner of her eye for a nanosecond then back to the head of the table where Allie's father was clinking his glass with a spoon. The room fell quiet, and Madden sat back, swallowing a sigh. It was not the time or place, but having Jacey disappointed in him *again* sat like a concrete block on his chest.

"I want to thank you all for celebrating with us. For a while, I wasn't sure my headstrong daughter would find someone she deemed worthy. But after getting to know Shane over the past year, I know she has. I'd like to go around the table and let everyone offer a few words to the couple. To Allie and Shane."

Everyone raised their glasses and drank, then they started with the speeches. Madden didn't mean to, but he kind of blanked out, watching his sister and willing her to acknowledge him. When she did, it was with annoyance. A small elbow jabbed him in the side. Saralynn. He frowned at her, but then it sunk in. The whole table was looking at him. Oops.

"Oh, sorry. Uh, Reese, you've become like another brother to me over the past couple years. You're a good guy, a good friend, and you deserve the best. And you found that in Allie. Seriously, does anyone know someone else who could put up with him? Hold on to her." Laughs and knowing looks all around eased some of the embarrassment, and Madden took a sip of water.

• • •

Perfect toast or not, Madden Vaughn was somewhere else. He lacked his usual finesse and was staring holes in Jacey. They must not have worked things out. Saralynn resisted the crazy urge to put a comforting hand on his arm and instead focused on her brother and her sister-to-be. "You looked out for me my whole life, big brother. I never thought a lot about love until I watched you fall for Allie. She brought out the best in you, and it made me want better for myself. Oh, and as far as your unofficial first date goes, you're welcome. To a lifetime of happiness."

Everyone laughed, raised glasses, and continued the speeches. She tried to listen, but for the life of her, she couldn't stop watching Madden fidget with his silverware. He *really* could not stand to be at odds with his sister. Yeah, the few times her sisters, Sophie and

Shiloh, wouldn't talk to her had been pretty miserable. Still. She couldn't remember ever wanting to comfort a *guy*. She'd always been the comfortee and usually as a means to get something.

After the final speech and applause, conversation picked back up as people finished their entrees. She poked Madden's foot with the toe of her pump, then cocked her head toward the door. Without waiting to see if he got the hint, she pushed her chair back and slipped into the hallway. Seconds ticked by, and she folded her arms and leaned against the wall. Those signals were universal, right?

The door opened, and he strode to her with a raised brow. Then he flashed that trademark smile, even if it was missing some wattage. "Was that code for 'Let's make out'?"

She rolled her eyes and dropped her arms. "You are not that dumb."

"So, no."

"*No*. I just wanted to talk to you because … it looks like you haven't talked to your sister."

"And you can't bear to see me upset? Saralynn, I'm shocked. You don't have a rep for being the nurturing type."

Her lips parted and scorching comebacks just begged for release, but she held them in check. No, she hadn't been known for caring about feelings. Honestly, it was a surprising plot twist for her, too, but she *did* care about his for some reason. He had this talent for drawing people in, and apparently sharing that talent didn't make one immune to it.

At least his feelings weren't the only reason she'd brought him out there. "Your relationship with Jacey is your business. It matters to me because I have to release a statement no later than Monday addressing that reporter's accusation against you. You said you didn't gamble. I need a little more than that."

The hard line of his jaw tightened, and he glanced through the windowed door at the party. "And you think now is a good time?"

"No, I don't. But you didn't come back to the office yesterday, and tomorrow will be an even worse time, and I don't have your cell number. Just a short explanation. Throw me a bone here."

Mischief tinted his eyes, and she cut him off with an accusing finger. "If you make one boner joke, you'll be wearing my crème brûlée by the end of the night."

"Jeez, lighten up." He lifted his palms in surrender but amusement remained on his face.

Lighten up. She'd never been on the receiving end of that before. Just how much *had* this job changed her? No time to worry about it now. "Look, my job is to protect you—the team. To protect the team. Please don't complicate my life." *Any more than you already have.*

His amusement turned thoughtful and sort of sweet, which was somehow worse. She squirmed inside, and she *never* squirmed. She used to be the squirm inducer. What the hell?

"Do you want my number?"

The notched-up smartass had pushed her last button. She set her hands on her hips so she wouldn't lunge for his throat.

Finally, he nodded. "Before the jousting show, a couple of the guys were playing craps. Not me. I hung back. Scotty won big and handed out chips. I put a couple in my jacket pocket."

Her eyes felt like they might pop out of their sockets. "If that's all it was, why didn't you clear this up earlier? You're totally innocent."

"Now I am. Problem is, I have a pretty long history of being guilty, so it's hard for Jace to believe anything else."

"But you can prove it. Scotty'll back you up. They all will. This is an easy fix … " The sadness and hurt on his face almost made her look away. The rumor, she could fix. But the damage was done and irreversible to the brother-sister bond. Even once Jacey knew the truth, it wouldn't take back the sting Madden felt now. Damn it, Saralynn wanted to hug him.

She felt helpless. It was a foreign emotion, and she was not a fan. More bewildering was why it bothered her so much. Madden represented the kind of meaningless flirtation she was trying to grow beyond. Why did she have the crazy urge to haul him against the wall and kiss that smile back onto his face?

He cleared his throat. "It's fine. We better get back."

It wasn't fine. Not yet.

Chapter Four

"Hope! It's not time for the flowers yet!" Shiloh nearly knocked Saralynn over chasing after her three-year-old daughter, who ran through the hotel suite screeching at an eardrum-piercing decibel as she threw rose petals all over the place.

Saralynn held her hands over her ears until the screaming stopped, then smoothed her dress and shook her head to clear it. *I love my niece. But I'm never going off the pill.* Dean, her nephew and the ring bearer, huddled under the desk, watching with wide eyes. At four years old, he was quiet and shy, the antithesis of Hope. Saralynn squatted down to his level. "Hey, buddy. Still got the rings?"

He nodded and held out a decorative pillow. Both rings were secured on top with satin ribbon.

"Good job. I'd hide under there with you if it wouldn't wrinkle my dress."

That earned a smile from him, and she winked before standing up again. Allie, the bride, stood in the middle of a three-sided mirror while Mac, her maid of honor, flitted around making sure dress, shoes, hair, and makeup were perfect. Sophie helped Shiloh wrangle Hope and pick up the strewn petals. Jacey sat alone on the couch, staring at her phone.

Really, it was none of Saralynn's business. Every brain cell voted to leave it alone. And yet, somehow, her feet were moving. When she stopped in front of the couch, Jacey looked up.

"Um ... " Saralynn licked her lips. "Do you mind if I ... ?" She gestured to the open cushion.

"No, please. Sit." Jacey scooted over and set her phone on the coffee table. "Crazy in here, huh?"

"Actually this is pretty normal for a Reese family get-together."

Jacey grinned, and Saralynn almost changed her mind. Then the image of Madden's beaten puppy face surfaced and steeled her reserve. "I uh … I don't mean to overstep, but I talked to Madden, and it was all a mistake. He didn't really gamble. Some of the other guys did, and they handed out chips. He put some in his pocket and forgot about them."

Jacey's smile slid off her face and was replaced with pity. "I know he can be very convincing. But that's a stretch, even for him."

"No, it's true. I asked the guys this morning, and they confirmed it."

"They're all friends. That doesn't surprise me."

For a second, shock prevented a reply. *Would* the guys lie for Madden? Would he have lied to her? His own sister seemed to think so. But it was hard to con a con, and she'd been no stranger to bending the truth in the past. It didn't feel like a lie. "I'll get the security tapes from the casino."

Jacey stared like she was waiting for the punch line, then arched a brow. "They don't just give those out."

"Let me worry about it."

"You really don't have to do this. We'll just tell the press he indulged a bit because of the bachelor party, but it was nothing big."

Except it *was* big to Madden. She'd seen his heart practically shatter in that hallway, and she didn't want to see it again. "Just trust me."

Before Jacey could respond, the wedding planner opened the suite door. "Okay, it's show time! Places, everyone."

• • •

Saralynn sat at the bridal party table sandwiched between her older sisters, who leaned around her to carry on a conversation. Shiloh talked nonstop about her kids, and when Sophie could get a word in, it was an offer to babysit. As much as Saralynn loved her nieces and nephews, the thought of braving the wild horde alone for more than one hour gave her hives. Guilt poked her in the ribs. "I would totally babysit, Shi, if I didn't live here now."

"Oh, I know, hon. We're just so proud of you." Back to baby talk. The maid of honor, Mac, jumped in enthusiastically about her toddler.

Saralynn leaned back and glanced around the ballroom. Her brother was dancing with her new sister, and he'd never looked happier. She smiled and bit the inside of her lip. No more crying. It had been all she could do in the ceremony to keep from sobbing into her bouquet. Reese's whole life had been hockey. It had taken Allie to make him realize what happy really was. He deserved it.

Groomsmen returned with drinks for everyone at the table. Madden placed a cosmo in front of her, studied her face, then held out his hand. She blinked. "What?"

"Come on. I know you've been asked to dance before."

Sophie looked up. "Hah. In high school, there was always a *line* to dance with her that stretched back to the bathroom."

Saralynn narrowed her eyes at her sister then slapped her hand into Madden's open palm and let him pull her up. He spun her around, and she couldn't help a smile. "This doesn't mean I like you."

"Oh, I know. But what kind of gentleman would I be if I didn't rescue a woman in need?"

"I didn't *need* rescuing."

"Coulda fooled me. Five more minutes of kiddie convo, and I bet you would have snapped. I saw you eyeing a butter knife."

She laughed as he swung her onto the dance floor and into his arms. "Smooth. So this was just suicide prevention."

"And you look really good in that dress."

"Ah-ha." Allie *had* been very kind to the bridesmaids, choosing a strapless, floor-length, shamrock dress that would flatter a boulder, and Saralynn was no boulder. Male attention was nothing new, but it felt like Madden wasn't looking *at* her. He was looking through her. Like he could see into her. It was distracting. No wonder he was so good at picking up women.

"What?" He raised his brows, innocence in his eyes.

"Not gonna happen. You're the boss's brother. I've only been on the job a year, but even I know it would be stupid to date you." Not to mention he didn't fit into the new plan. No more cheap flirting. No more smiling at guys for free drinks or leading them on when she had trouble remembering their names. That wasn't her anymore. She'd only help him because it was her job.

"It would be stupid, but you're oh-so-drawn to my subtle charm anyway." He guided her closer, and the hand on her hip moved to her lower back. Her cheek touched his shoulder, and while her head said to pull back, the rest of her wasn't listening. He might be a little right. That didn't mean he needed to know.

"You're subtle like Reese's gym bag after practice."

His lips brushed her ear. "You saying I smell like your brother's sweaty hockey equipment?"

No. In fact, he smelled like new leather and the citrus-ocean scent of Ralph Lauren's Polo Sport. "I'm saying I know your game because I used to play it. But I don't anymore. And I don't date co-workers." She expected a quick comeback as was his usual style, but he fell quiet and swayed with her to the impersonator singing a convincing Sinatra. "I've Got You Under My Skin." How appropriate. "No denials?"

He tilted his head and held her gaze for a minute. "Why? You seem to have me figured out."

Didn't she? Could there be more to Madden Vaughn than a hot bod and a reputation? *It doesn't matter.* "Tell me you were being serious last night. The other guys gambled, but you didn't."

His face went blank, betrayed by the wounded look in his eyes, but only for a second. "I didn't."

She managed not to wince, but it felt like she was the one whipping the puppy now. If he was lying, he was a world-class sociopath. And she didn't believe that. "Okay. Then I'm going to clear your name. To everybody."

• • •

Madden lifted his chin and looked down at the Victoria's Secret model in his arms. Okay, maybe she wasn't one, but a single audition would be all it took. The sexiness was only made more potent by the girlish resemblance to Samantha from *Who's the Boss.* She'd been off-limits since the day he met her. Not just because they worked together, but because Reese had held a group meeting when she started and put out a threat to anyone who went near her. So he'd hung back. That didn't mean he hadn't looked up every time she passed in the hallway or had the occasional fantasy.

Holding her gave him a lot more to work with, except now he knew fantasy would never live up to the real thing. And for some reason, she wanted to help him. "Why? It's not just because it's your job." Her wide, whiskey brown eyes sparked, and he cut off a denial. "Uh-uh. If you can read me, I can read you. We play the same game, remember?"

"I don't play anymore."

"Who says I do? Doesn't mean we don't remember the rules."

She studied him as they swayed around the floor, and he returned the favor. Finally, she sighed and lifted a shoulder. "I don't know, okay? I see how much it hurts that Jacey doesn't believe you, and I happen to think you're innocent. I know what it's like when your family doesn't always believe the best about you."

"And you *care*." Meant as an observation, not an accusation, but he could rub it in a little.

She scoffed, though there wasn't much conviction behind it. When it was clear he didn't buy her indignation, it drained from her expression. "Okay, fine. What if I do?"

Needling her was fun. He hadn't really expected a genuine reply. A response escaped him. "Then I guess … I'm pretty lucky."

Her gaze dropped to his mouth before darting back to his eyes.

What did she want? Was she torturing him on purpose? "I've seen what you can do. Wouldn't want to be on the bad side of a mastermind." The song ended, and he kissed the back of her hand in a half-bow. "Thanks for the dance."

Her lips parted as he disappeared into the crowd.

The look on her face just before he'd walked away was priceless. Not that they had any kind of future. She was a co-worker. A smokin' hot co-worker, but Vegas was full of pretty faces. Except there was something else. Under her back-off attitude, there were traces of a vulnerable girl, and he got the feeling not many other people were allowed to see that. Not just because of her own walls but because of her brother, the brick wall, who would stand between her and any potential suitor.

She wanted to clear his name. With Jacey. God, how long had it been since anyone had complete faith in him? She trusted him. Believed him. Maybe she just didn't know him well enough, but it felt incredible. Humbling. Suddenly, Jacey wasn't the only one he wanted to prove himself to.

Stop it, man. Not gonna happen. Now to fight the part of him wired to take that as a challenge.

Chapter Five

Sunday, February 23rd

Saralynn hung her coat in the closet then darted around her apartment, picking up here and there. Not that she left the place a mess, but one couldn't be too careful when company was armed with a psych degree. Actually, several degrees. She and Allie had both come from the arena, so it wasn't a huge surprise when the buzzer rang a minute later. "It's open!"

Allie let herself in and looked around. "You really customized this since I saw it last."

Saralynn grabbed a bottle of wine from the counter and snagged two glasses on her way to the living room. "Oh, yeah. In the time I've actually been here. I feel like I live at work. Not that I'm complaining."

"Preaching to the choir, sister." Allie tucked her coat on the back of a kitchen chair then took a seat on the couch.

"That's right; you *are* my sister now. How cool is that? Sucks that your honeymoon was delayed."

Allie accepted a glass, pulled the cork, and poured for both of them. "It's no big deal. Comes with marrying a professional athlete. We're thinking the Maldives in July."

"So jealous." Saralynn sipped and willed the alcohol to work faster. Unfortunately, liquid courage took its time, so she'd have to find some of the real stuff.

Allie swirled the wine in her glass. A quiet minute passed, then another. When it got almost painful, she broke the silence. "So … I'm guessing this has to do with Madden Vaughn."

Saralynn's heart beat hard and fast, and she took a big gulp. "Why do you say that?" Because she knew, that's why. Allie knew everything about everyone. It was the woman's trademark. Why even continue to question it?

"I heard about the trouble he's in, and I know it's your job to deal with it. I saw the way you two looked at each other during the rehearsal dinner and at the reception, not to mention that dance. And then you catch me right after today's game and ask me to stop by. The only part I haven't figured out is why you didn't call Shiloh or Sophie. They're in town until tomorrow."

God, she felt like a guilty kid every time she talked to Allie, even if she hadn't done anything. But the girl was good. And that's what she needed. "I love my sisters, but you actually listen when other people talk. You don't harbor any lingering resentment for boyfriends I may or may not have stolen in the past or popularity that really had nothing to do with me. And you know how to keep a secret. I mean, it's your job, right? Please tell me you were the only one who noticed—"

"You and the lost Backstreet Boy? Yeah, pretty sure it was just me. You know if Shane picked up on it, he'd be here threatening to lock you in your room until you're forty."

If that wasn't the truth. She shuddered and finished her glass. It was weird hearing someone call her brother anything but Reese, a rule he'd laid down in peewee hockey, but it was nice, too. "I just turned twenty-three, and he thinks I'm still five."

"You will always be his baby sister. It doesn't help that you look like you're sixteen."

"You're my new favorite. Don't tell Reese."

Allie laughed and gave her a high five. "Okay. Now what's going on with Madden?"

Saralynn fell back against the couch and stared at the little chandelier dripping in neon pink crystals above them. "That reporter is his ex, and I guess there's a lot of bad blood there, so she took a low shot. But he swears to me he didn't gamble.

Jacey thinks he did. She wants me to release a statement tomorrow downplaying it as a bachelor party thing."

"That wouldn't be so bad for the team's image."

"No ... "

"But you believe him. You don't think he did it, and you want to help."

"Right."

Allie cringed. "I know you, and your scheming scares me. What are you gonna do?"

"I'm going to get the casino security footage. You probably don't want to know how. What do you call it? Plausible deniability."

"Oh God."

Saralynn laughed. "I'm kidding. About the last part." Mostly. So far her plan involved a bribe of free game tickets and a low-cut shirt.

"So if you've got it all figured out, I must be here for something else. Maybe you're not sure *why* you're doing all this."

Saralynn blew out a hard breath and poured herself another glass.

Allie nodded in a knowing way that would be annoying if she weren't the answer-keeper. "I'll put it in layman's terms. You *like* him."

"I have a lot of experience liking guys. This is so not that. In fact, he—"

"Drives you completely crazy because he reminds you of yourself? Before you ask, I know because I just did that dance with your brother. And look how that turned out."

Saralynn swatted at her sister-in-law's knee. "He's like the *old* me. I used to be ... self-centered. I used to look at people and think about what they could give me. But that's not me anymore. I meant my toast at the dinner. And Madden, by all accounts, is Peter Pan. He's a few years from thirty, but he's still a hopeless flirt with poor impulse control. And if Jacey's right, if he really did gamble ... "

"Then he fooled you, and you can't trust him."

"If he fooled me, *nobody* can trust him. My lie detector's even better than yours. I just don't understand why it even *matters* to me."

"He could represent the perfect challenge. You used to enjoy the game of getting a guy to fall for you, right? Well, here's one who's not such an easy mark. He's on your level, and that can be pretty irresistible. Believe me. Or you might be projecting. You want to believe the best about him because you want to believe the best about yourself. Or maybe you see some redeeming quality in him and think he could be a really good man."

Saralynn's temples ached, and she rubbed her forehead. "I don't know which possibility is worse. I thought I was going to feel better after talking to you."

Allie gave her a sympathetic half-smile. "Sorry. I don't come with that guarantee. I do come with an opinion. When you meet someone who gives you a feeling you can't define, you owe it to yourself to figure it out. Don't judge Madden before you really know him. Good and bad. Just ... be careful given the circumstances. And keep me updated. How am I doing as a sister?"

"You could give Shi and Sophie lessons. Me, too." They clinked glasses, and Saralynn took a long drink. She'd need it to brave the next morning.

Chapter Six

Madden walked into work with a smile. It lasted approximately three point five seconds before the door to his sister's office opened and she hooked a finger at him. Her face looked as stormy as she ever let it, and the latte curdled in his stomach. *But I didn't do anything.* That thought should have been comforting, but that mix of disappointment and anger in Jacey's eyes triggered reflex guilt from all the times he *had* done something.

He followed her inside and closed the door. "Jace … I don't know what's wrong, but I just want to thank you for believing me. That statement in the paper today—"

"Wasn't from me. It wasn't the one I issued." There was a trace of regret in her tone, but disapproval still reigned.

"If you didn't … then who?" But he knew as soon as the words left his mouth. Saralynn went to bat for him. It hadn't been just talk. Warmth spread in his chest, and he felt a little lightheaded. Those things dimmed when Jacey's expression didn't change and her words sunk in. *She* still didn't believe him. What hurt more was knowing that if her husband had gotten to the party early enough to be at those tables, Carter's word would have been all it took to change her mind.

"Maddie, you know I want to believe you were just standing there while the other guys gambled. But … "

"But that doesn't sound like me, does it?" There was no anger in his voice, and he tried to hold back the hurt but didn't do a good job judging by the glossy, just-held-in-check tears in his sister's eyes.

She looked away and cleared her throat. "I have to ask. Is there something going on with you and Saralynn? I saw you at the reception. And then she went ahead with the release denying Linden's accusation."

"What? No. Maybe she just believed me."

When Jacey met his eyes again, she flashed a brief, amused smile and shook her head. "You are really good at pulling people in. I'm not saying you used her, but maybe she got caught in the Madden tractor beam."

"Are you kidding? My mojo doesn't work on her, Jace. Maybe hers cancels it out. I don't know. From what Reese said back when she started, she's the one used to wrapping men around her finger. She doesn't get wrapped. So to speak."

"I just don't think it would be a good idea—"

The door whooshed open behind him, and Saralynn skidded in, out of breath. She held up a flash drive. "Sorry. Sorry I'm late. And before you fire me for releasing that statement, you need to see this."

Jacey hesitated as if she couldn't pick which response to go with. Finally, she stepped back and made room in front of the computer on her desk. Saralynn scooted around and plugged in the device. A few clicks, and a silent video played. Madden leaned over to see. Casino footage. Reese, Scott, Cole, and a couple other guys stood around the craps table. And there he was, behind them, hands in his pockets. The whole time.

Jacey's shoulders slumped just slightly, and she closed her eyes.

"I know I'm way overstepping," Saralynn said, standing straight. "I shouldn't have released anything without your okay, and I won't ever again if you don't fire me on the spot. But at least you know no one will come forward with anything contradictory." Balls. The girl had steel balls. When Jacey didn't reply, Saralynn lowered her chin. Just a notch. "I'll be in my office."

She slid by him, and he breathed in something light and sweet like cotton candy with an undertone of vanilla. When she left, Jacey hung her head, her hands curled over the back of her leather desk chair. "I'm sorry, Maddie."

He nodded but couldn't think of anything to say. Yeah, now she knew, but it had taken video proof—his word wasn't enough. And maybe it never would be. That hurt almost as much as knowing it was his fault. "It's okay, sis. One time out of a hundred, right? I can't blame you for playing the odds."

She looked even more fragile than he felt. It broke his heart. "Jace?"

Her face closed down, and that weakness was replaced by impenetrable resolve.

"Everything's okay now. Right?"

"I'm pregnant."

He rocked back, numb with shock. Pregnant. He would have a niece or nephew. Happiness and excitement rocketed through him until tears welled in his sister's eyes then rolled down her cheeks, and she wouldn't look at him.

"How long have you known?"

She grabbed a tissue from her desk and wiped her face. "About a week."

A week. "Why didn't you tell me?"

"I didn't want it to overshadow the wedding." That might've been true, but they'd gotten so close the past two years. She told him whenever she got her hair cut.

"That's not the only reason."

Her lips quivered. She pressed them together and looked at her lap. "I've been doing a lot of thinking. I know this rumor about you wasn't true, but it's like my whole life changed when I took that test. I need to do what's right for my child. Make the right choices. I need to know you'll be a positive influence. You know how much I love you." Her tears returned, and she balled the tissue hard in her hand. "I'm just not sure you're there yet."

The room went blurry around the edges, and he tried to focus. "Are you saying you don't want me involved in the kid's life?"

"No. I don't know. Please understand—"

"I don't understand. All these years, you never gave up on me, not even when I deserved it. I'm finally turning my life around, finally *earning* that faith, and now you're pushing me away?"

"Madden, how many times have you turned your life around?" The soft, careful tone of her voice drove the words home instead of making him defensive. How many times *had* he said that? Too many.

"But it's true this time. You've seen it. You know."

Her pained smile wavered. "Maybe. I hope it's true. But this isn't the first time, and I was wrong before."

You can trust me. I'm different. The words were on the tip of his tongue, but she was right. He'd said them so often they'd lost meaning. "What can I do to prove it to you?"

"I don't know. I think proof only comes with time."

"Then at least give me the chance to show you. Please?"

She stared at him, expressionless, for a minute but finally nodded. "Okay. But I'm serious. I have to do what's best for the baby."

"I know. I won't let you down. Either of you."

• • •

Saralynn sat behind her desk with her head in her hands. What had she done? She didn't jump first and ask questions on the way down. Not anymore. But she'd just thrown away the best thing that had ever happened to her, and why? What did Allie say? Madden was the perfect challenge. Except challenges were about winning, and she'd potentially lost everything.

Next on the list of motivations?

She wanted to believe the best about him because she wanted to believe the best about herself. Nah. Her best self wouldn't dive under a bus for a guy she barely knew.

Moving on.

Madden had some redeeming quality and deep down was a good man. Well, he hadn't lied. This time. And ...

The door swung open, and her heart fell into her Jimmy Choos. Not the boss. Just the devil. With a smile like a toothpaste ad. He closed the door and leaned against the knob for a second like he was afraid someone else would come in. "Uh ... I can't believe you—"

"I know. Neither can I. Out-of-body experience is the best I got. I should probably start boxing my things."

"No. It's okay. I mean, it's not. You can't go behind Jace's back like that in the future, but you're not fired."

"I'm *not?*" Before she could formulate another question, the answer danced in front of her with a baton. "You asked her not to."

"Least I could do after everything you did for me. What *did* you do anyway? How'd you get that footage?"

Heat flooded her cheeks followed by shock socking her in the gut. When had she ever been embarrassed about using her wiles to get what she wanted? What did it matter if he knew? "I explained the importance the video had to the team."

"And when that wasn't enough?"

"I might have thrown in some front row tickets."

He arched his brows.

"And left a few buttons undone. Happy?"

His gaze dropped to the cleavage exposed by those buttons, and the corner of his mouth quirked up. She was two seconds from smacking him when he met her eyes. The vulnerability there, the openness, froze her to the spot. "Thank you. Seriously. You don't know how much it means. You defended me before you even knew for yourself I was innocent."

Her guard wavered, lowered, and she dipped her head. That gaze was too intense. "I knew. You don't have to thank me."

"Yes, I do." The intent was right there in his voice, but somehow she was still surprised when he stepped around the desk, lifted her chin with one finger, and kissed her softly, sweetly. When he leaned back, he looked as surprised as she was, but he covered it with a grin.

She licked her lips and tried to regain control of her pulse. "You have a pretty high opinion of yourself if you think that covers it." But dear God, it just about did.

He laughed, and seeing the weight leave his broad shoulders cleared his tab. Not that she'd ever tell him that. He backed up a step. "You're right. I owe you dinner at least."

"Oh, no. You don't have to—"

"Want to. Wednesday night, you name the place."

A million reasons to say no tumbled through her mind. What came out was "Lotus of Siam—meet you at eight."

Chapter Seven

Wednesday, February 26th

A strip mall. Of all the high-end, over-the-top places to eat in Vegas, Saralynn Reese had chosen a strip mall. The same Saralynn who came to work in so many labels the designers should've paid her an advertising fee. Madden sat in his Escalade and slid a hand over his jaw. It had to be a joke. She wouldn't show. Indecision held him in place a few more seconds. His stomach growled. Date or no date, he needed dinner. He hauled himself out and locked the car with a beep, feeling self-conscious in a lot full of late-model sedans.

The inside of Lotus of Siam looked a *lot* different. Rows of polished wooden tables gleamed under low, warm lighting, and the dark green carpet was a little faded but clean. It had a homey feel. And seated in the back, legs crossed and foot bobbing, sat Saralynn, twirling the straw in her water. The top half of her light brown hair was scooped up away from her face and secured with red chopsticks while the back half hung in loose curls over her shoulders. She wore a sleeveless, see-through white shirt with a red tank underneath and skintight white pants that ended just past her knees. But those shoes—shiny red, strappy sandals with spike heels—caught his attention. Feet had held no special fascination for him before, but those shoes had him subtly adjusting himself on the way over.

"This place is not what I was expecting." He sat across from her at the small table for two against a mirrored wall.

She wiggled her toes painted the same red as the shoes and shook her head at him. "If you always judge things by how they look, you might miss out on something great. It took me a while to learn that one. But now I'm taking chances on new experiences."

That observation struck deep. Most people judged him on the surface. To be fair, very few got to see underneath. The same seemed to be true for her. He weighed the pros and cons of asking if he fit into the new experiences category, but no sense pushing his luck. It was a huge surprise she'd said yes to begin with, and what the hell had inspired the invitation anyway? Had to be that kiss, the one on loop in his head. Dinner opened up the possibility for another. Jacey had just finished telling him what a bad idea it would be to get too close to Saralynn, he'd just promised not to let his sister down, and practically the next thing he did was ask Saralynn on a date. As far as he'd come from his impulse-prone former self, apparently he still had a ways to go.

Every line in his arsenal seemed like it would fall flat with the vixen in front of him. When in doubt, compliment. "I'm all for new experiences. And I have to say, you look incredible tonight."

She smiled, then appeared to catch herself and gave him a wary stare. "Just so we're clear, this is a thank-you dinner. Not a date."

If that were true, what did she wear on a real date? The possibilities weren't exactly the cold shower he needed. Their server, an Asian woman wearing a cross between an Indian sari and a Japanese kimono, appeared and asked for their order.

Saralynn went first. "I'll have the drunken noodle sea bass."

Madden blinked and glanced at the menu. He'd never had Thai before and with only time to skim, half the offerings were a mystery. "Uh, that sounds good. I'll have the same." The server giggled and fanned her lashes at him. Her cheerful nod almost looked like a small bow before she left, and then they were alone again.

"Seriously?"

"What?"

"That waitress was practically fawning all over you. Are there pheromones in your cologne or something?"

Could it be? He grinned. "Hey, I didn't do anything. And if this isn't a date, why would you be jealous?"

"I'm *not* jealous."

"There's certainly no reason for it. You're the most gorgeous woman in this room."

"Yeah, okay. Will you turn it off, please? I'd like to have dinner with my co-worker. Not a reality TV host."

Ouch. No one had ever called him out like that. Combined with the co-worker classification, things weren't looking good. No problem. Just time to regroup. "Okay. On this not-a-date, would it be all right to ask you about yourself?"

• • •

Saralynn leaned back in her chair and studied the man across from her wearing a bright blue crew-neck T-shirt with an oversized purple plaid pattern on the shoulders under a streamlined navy blazer. Not his most casual look, but bolder than his office clothes. If she wasn't mistaken, this was date Madden. As formal as he got outside of a wedding or funeral. Somehow, it still said *polished*. Maybe because that T-shirt was probably just under $200.

He thought this was a date. Hard to deny that when she'd spent two hours getting ready after work. Her plan had been an old hockey tee, beat-up jeans, and sneakers, with a full ponytail. But God help her, she couldn't leave the apartment like that when she imagined how good he'd look. The only compromise was putting half her hair up. Then the devil on her shoulder suggested the sexy chopsticks, and her last good intention came crumbling down.

Now here they were, dressed up on their not-a-date, and he wanted to test boundaries. This was a dangerous game, but as long as they didn't cross the line … "I guess a few questions would be okay."

The line of his shoulders relaxed a little, and he sipped the water she'd ordered for him. "I better make them good then. Tell me about what it was like growing up with Reese."

She smiled reflexively then frowned at him in suspicion. That was the second time he'd drawn one from her so fast. He was good. "By the time I was five, he was ten, and hockey took up most of his time. I remember only about four good years with him before he went with Carter to a school in Minnesota. But he was my protector even when I didn't want him to be. I was closer to him than my sisters. Still am. I was kind of a tomboy until my teens when I … blossomed."

"Into one hell of a rose."

"Thanks, but I'm more remembered for my thorns."

His light blue eyes widened in a silent "Do tell."

She picked at a straw wrapper on the table. "That stuff's not important."

"You think *I'm* going to judge you?"

The corner of her mouth twitched, and she flattened her hands in her lap. "Okay, fine. Things came easily to me in high school. I was cheer captain and queen of every dance. I had a big group of followers but not a single friend. Not a real one. Guys were interested but assholes. So by the time I got to college, I stopped caring if they cared. I casually dated my way through the next four years and none of them even stand out in my mind. It wasn't until I started working for the team that I saw how different things could be. How different I could be. And I never want to go back."

Whoa. None of that was supposed to spill out, but once the leak sprung, she couldn't stop. She pressed her lips together and stared at the flickering tea light in the middle of the table.

"I can't say I know exactly how you feel. My experience was a little different. But I think the keynotes are the same."

That shouldn't be a surprise given the last few days, but somehow it was. Most people couldn't relate to her "charmed" life. Most people didn't know the curse of it. Hell, neither had she—not really—until recently. For the first time, she met a date's gaze and actually wanted to hear what he had to say.

He looked a little surprised by the opening, and she bit the inside of her cheek to hold back another smile. Madden took a sip of his water. "Oh, okay. Well, I wasn't enough of a joiner to be prom king, but I had my share of dates in high school. I got serious with a girl in college, but it turned out she wasn't that serious about me. And I guess you now know everything there is to know about the Linden thing."

Saralynn did her best not to flinch. The Linden thing. She'd done some Google stalking. Being fully informed was part of her job, and she couldn't manage his media situation without knowing all the facts. "Yeah, what's up with that? What did you *see* in her? Not that I'm qualified to throw rocks, but she sounds kind of evil from what I read."

He looked down, tilted his head to one side, and chewed on his lower lip. She beat down the stupid urge to kiss it better. She'd hit a sore spot, but to his credit, he didn't withdraw. When he met her eyes again, that trademark twinkle was tempered by regret, embarrassment, and just a little pain.

"That's a good question. I've asked myself that a lot. Definitely not one of my proudest achievements. I don't know. At first, I guess I was swayed by appearance and attitude. She didn't back down, and she went after what she wanted. And she really seemed to be into me. I thought we were starting something, but then she used me to get dirt on my sister. She apologized, but it didn't mean anything. I thought about her from time to time, but I was finally letting go. And then I saw the wedding announcement."

The server returned with their order. After assuring the woman they didn't need anything else, she left them alone again. Saralynn dug in to her dish, eating the greens off the top first. Some kind of reassurance seemed appropriate after his story, but that had never been one of her strong points. Best to let the moment pass. And she would have if she hadn't glimpsed him pushing around his noodles, not out of distaste, but discontent.

"You know, she's not the one who got away. She's a bullet you were lucky to dodge. Seriously. And this is coming from a former hollow-point. You're not still hung up on her, are you? Not that I'm interested."

His sad expression broke and crumbled away with a laugh and a grin that dropped her guard. "Of course you're not. I've been thinking about that night. It wasn't that I wanted to marry her or ruin her wedding. I guess it just sucked that she'd been decent enough to another guy that they'd made it down the aisle. I must not be that much of a prize."

"You're hard on yourself."

"Said the pot to the kettle. I don't think you're as bad as you think you are, either. Maybe we should give a real date a shot."

It felt so good to hear him say that. Too good. Was this what she wanted? Validation that she wasn't as bad as she used to be? That she might be capable of something more? It didn't take Allie's psych degrees to know those things couldn't come from another person. She played it off with a smile. "You don't want to get involved with me. I'm 'relationship napalm' according to my brother."

"Reese said that? Not very nice."

"No, it's not. But it is accurate. Or it was. I'm a work in progress."

Madden spread his arms in a "Hello, me, too" gesture.

"Okay, yeah, but that's why we can't date. Ever hear of the blind leading the blind?"

"Or maybe we could encourage each other. Come on, who else fits this specific support group?" He was tenacious, she'd give him that. And exasperating. Before she could come up with a response, he poked again at his food. "So where are the noodles?"

Avoiding rejection with a change of topic. Her mouth dropped open in a mix of amusement and admiration. When he looked at her innocently, brows up, she sighed. "The slimy things on the bottom that look like squid? Those are noodles."

"Man." He made a face like a little kid looking at a plate of wilted broccoli. "You should write the menu descriptions."

"They're good. Try them." As encouragement, she took a forkful from her plate and licked her lips. "Mmmm."

He watched her mouth, and his Adam's apple bobbed. "You're giving me other ideas."

She pointed her fork at him. "Eat." But now that he'd brought it up, those other ideas danced around her head, too. Maybe it was the forbidden aspect, or maybe there really was something about him, but she couldn't remember wanting someone the way she wanted Madden Vaughn. It just wasn't going to happen.

His shoulders drooped dramatically, and he pouted, which only made him cuter, damn it. But he picked up his fork and tried a bite. Then another. "Hey, you're right. This is good."

"Yeah. I come here once a week. Not just for the food but the atmosphere."

"I can see that. This place isn't so ... Vegas."

"Exactly." She ate some sea bass and watched him wrestle a piece of his out from between the greens and the noodles. Adorable.

She was screwed.

Chapter Eight

Friday, February 28th

The main concourse of the Las Vegas arena teemed with fans eating, laughing, waiting for autographs, and playing carnival-style, hockey-themed games. So far so good. Saralynn clutched a glittery clipboard to her chest and navigated the pregame party in four-inch heels. She made her way to a long folding table decked out in black, green, and silver with a banner that read: Sinners' Den Fan Zone. People huddled around to buy player buttons, trading cards, Sinners Mardi Gras beads, and themed leis. The volunteer behind the table gave her a thumbs up, and she checked it off on her list.

"Update. Mic's all set up if you want to say a few words."

Her shoulders twitched at her assistant's voice in her Bluetooth earpiece. No matter how often she wore it, there was still that jack-in-the-box surprise every time someone said something. "Coming." She spotted the small stage in the middle of the concourse and maneuvered her way through the masses. On the way, she tousled her loose curls to cover the battery box on her glow horns headband and amped up her media smile.

She stepped up to the microphone on stage, and the crowd cheered. Pride bubbled up, but it wasn't like being voted this or that at a dance. They weren't applauding her. They were applauding the event she'd put together, and somehow that felt even better. "Thank you for coming to the party. We're glad to have you! Who's having a good time?" The responding roar almost made her wish for earplugs. "That's what I like to hear! Are you excited for the game?" They cheered louder, and a few whistles rang out. "All right! Don't forget to snag some Sinners swag, and it's not too late to enter the raffle for the signed jerseys. Let's go, Vegas!"

The music turned back up, absorbing the enthusiastic screams of agreement. Her smile faltered as she turned for the steps and saw Madden watching her from the mini rink with faux ice they'd set up for the kids. Her traitorous pulse picked up. The smart thing would be to ignore him, focus on her checklist. Except she'd just finished the list, and the event was running like a well-oiled machine. *Balls.*

Since their not-a-date, she'd only brushed by him in the hallway. When he was in his office, it was to talk with player agents behind a closed door. The trade deadline was right around the corner, so that made sense. It wasn't like he was avoiding her. Right? Not that she cared either way, but if there was avoiding to be done, she had dibs.

Curiosity got the best of her. Or maybe it was the way he still hadn't taken his eyes off her even as pint-sized hellions sprinted around him with inflatable hockey sticks. It wasn't until they started pelting him with little plastic pucks that his attention shifted. It was wrong to laugh. It was also involuntary. She covered it with a cough.

She leaned a hip against the mini rink wall and rested an elbow atop it. A box of plastic referee whistles sat on the ledge. She snagged one and blew hard, sounding an ear-splitting shriek. The munchkins abandoned their attack on Madden and resumed trying to score goals in the small nets.

"I had it under control." But he was not very convincing as he rubbed his legs and barely kept a straight face.

"Oh, sure. I just know how big of a kid *you* can be, and I figured it was only a matter of time until they elected you their leader. Then it'd be a short hop and skip to *Lord of the Flies.*"

"Flattery will get you everywhere." He ambled up to the wall and still beat her height by a few inches even with her killer heels.

"What are you doing here, anyway? You weren't on the volunteer list."

"I know, but I figured it'd be good to be a part of this. Attach myself to the team in a positive, public way."

He was right. That was a smart move. So why did she feel let down?

"And maybe I wanted to see you in action."

Boom, pleasure replaced the fallen feeling. How annoying was that? *I am not supposed to like you.* "Oh yeah? And?"

"You don't disappoint. You've been buzzing around this place like a squirrel on Red Bull. Aside from the tiny insurrection just a few minutes ago, everything's run like clockwork."

She started to smile then caught the last part of that. "Hey, how was the insurrection my fault?"

"You distracted me." His gaze darted down her body then back up, hot as a laser.

That probably worked on a lot of women. She wasn't completely unaffected, but he'd have to try a lot harder to find a line she hadn't heard. Or invented herself. "Right. Well, you might not want to turn your back on them for too long." She lifted her chin toward the corner where a couple of boys were wrestling on the faux ice.

"Oh, sh—crap. Hey, the game starts in half an hour. Can we talk then? Meet you in the owner's box?"

"Won't your sister and brother-in-law be there?"

"Nah, they watch by the players' entrance at ice level. Sometimes we invite friends or family, but it's empty tonight."

Such a bad idea. "Okay ... to talk."

"Right. Talk." His Cheshire Cat smile hinted otherwise and made her stomach flip flop as she watched him break up the future hockey players.

She replayed that kiss from the other day in her office for the hundredth time. It was so gentle. So innocent. And followed by the fantasy of throwing him down on her desk and peeling his clothes off with her teeth.

Bad Saralynn.

Why did bad have to be so fun?

· · ·

Even while keeping the peace among a swarm of kids under ten, all Madden could think about was getting some alone time with Saralynn. Now he paced the owner's box, stopped, and sat facing the ice, then turned around to sit on the table so he could watch the door. Talking to women had never fazed him before. Now his mouth was dry as all the moisture in his body seemed to go to his palms, and his heart was beating like he'd just had three espressos.

Saralynn was different but unnervingly familiar. She was immune to his best moves. Hell, she nearly made him want to give honesty a shot. She wasn't like any woman he'd met, but so many things about her matched up with his own personality blueprint.

One date was not enough. The more he got to know her, the more he wanted to know. He'd just brushed the surface Wednesday night, then spent Thursday and the better part of today trying to think about anything else. That plan had no chance. Especially not after Carter stepped in and took over the meetings with player agents. It had seemed a little off at first—they usually tag-teamed those things—but Carter liked to be hands-on as much as he could. Plus it gave Madden more time to think up the perfect date with Saralynn. Jace wouldn't be happy if she knew. Maybe she didn't need to know right away.

The door cracked open a sliver then eased the rest of the way, and Saralynn paused, staring past him through the window wall into the arena.

"It's okay. Everybody's watching the game. I just thought it would be quiet in here, and it's right down the hall from the press box. Figured you'd want to stop by there anyway and make sure the snacks were stocked. Those reporters love their pretzels."

She stepped inside and closed the door with a smirk. "You know me inside and out, huh?"

No, but I'd like to. "I'm a good guesser." He pulled two chairs to face each other and sat in one, then lounged back with an ankle crossed over his knee. If he looked relaxed, maybe she would be.

Saralynn set her clipboard on the table, unbuttoned her blazer, then sat with her legs crossed. Even in a pantsuit, she made him sweat. The green satin tank with black lace around the low, v-shaped neckline added to the effect. And because those red, strappy sandals remained emblazoned in his mind, he let his gaze travel down her legs to find shiny black pumps with a red sole. God help him.

"You wanted to talk."

Her voice snapped him back to the moment, and he met her eyes. How could someone look innocent and arrogant at the same time? It was sexy as hell. "Right. I was thinking … " *I can't get you out of my mind. Let's find an Elvis officiant at the Chapel of Love and figure the rest out later.* Nope. Couldn't go with that. He sighed. "Look, I don't know what to say to you. I'm usually smoother than this, but I keep getting the feeling that your arsenal is bigger than mine, so I'm just gonna lay it out there. You took a chance on me. You believed in me and put yourself on the line. And I can't help feeling like there could really be something here. I think you feel it, too, and I want to find out. What do you say to a date-date?"

Shell-shocked would be the best way to describe how she stared at him. Was she even breathing? She blinked, long lashes brushing her cheeks once. Twice. "If we're seen out together, things could get complicated."

"Feel free to correct me, but things are already complicated."

She picked at the lace hem of her shirt. "I love this job."

"I don't want you to feel pressured. You say no, we go on with business as usual. You're good for this team. I just had to ask because it would be too big of a regret if I didn't."

She pursed her lips and narrowed her eyes, but there was a playfulness to it. "Honest and vulnerable. That's a pretty bold move."

"What, guys have never played those cards with you before?"

"Oh, no. They've played them a lot. It just never worked before."

Muted screaming filtered through the glass wall, and he glanced over to see the Sinners celebrating a goal down on the ice. The feeling carried through him as he focused on the last thing she said. "You admit you like me."

A smile flickered at the corners of her full lips. "You're not what I expected."

"Is that good or bad?"

"I'll let you know."

He unfolded his legs and sat up. "Does that mean you'll go out with me?"

She opened her mouth but hesitated.

"What if I said I had an idea that would let us go out in public but be alone in one of the coolest places you've ever seen?"

"That sounds like a riddle, and I'd say you were making it up to get me to say yes."

"I swear it's real. Do you have a camera? Other than your phone?"

"I … " She closed her eyes for a beat then nodded. "Yeah, I guess. Where are you going with this?"

"You'll see. The team doesn't play again until Monday. Pick you up tomorrow night at seven thirty?" The words came out rapid-fire despite his attempts to stay cool. Maybe the confusing blitz would catch her off guard enough to agree.

"This is pretty elaborate for a last-minute thing, unless you already made the plans. You were so sure I'd say yes?"

"Not even a little bit."

"Okay. Out of sheer curiosity."

"I'll take it."

Chapter Nine

Saturday, March 1st

Wear sneakers. One two-word text a half hour before he was supposed to pick her up, and now she had to rethink her whole outfit. Sneakers. Where the hell were they going? Saralynn flipped through hangers in her closet as fast as she could. If heels were out, a dress probably was too. The buzzer rang. *Shit! What kind of guy is on time?* The dress would have to do. A floral sundress was casual enough. She slid a faded denim vest over it and wedged her bare feet into pink Converse shoes without untying the laces.

She was halfway out of her bedroom before she turned on her tiptoes and darted back to the bed to pick up her camera. She stuffed the thing into her wristlet purse and jogged out the apartment door, nearly coming nose to chest with Madden. "You're early."

He checked his watch. "It's seven thirty on the dot."

"You're a guy. You're supposed to be fifteen minutes late. Didn't you read the manual?"

He started to smile, but it wavered when she kept a straight face. "I'm … sorry? Always was a skimmer. Guess I need to study. I'll do better next time."

Why did he have to be so cute? Tonight's ensemble was typical Madden. Dark and faded but expensive jeans, a fitted, black *Vegas Is for Lovers* T-shirt, and some Doc Marten boots. Okay, those were a little unusual. "We're not going for a hike in the desert, are we?"

"Not exactly."

"What is 'not exactly'? I'm not a pee-behind-a-tree kind of girl."

"Oh, you're not? I couldn't tell."

Hands on hips, she engaged him in a staring contest. Only he was all too happy to participate according to the twinkle in his eyes. Finally, he cracked. "Look, I promise we'll be surrounded by electricity. And not just what's between us."

All right, that was pretty impressive. She smiled and swatted at his flat stomach, then sidestepped him and headed for his car. She climbed into the passenger side of his Escalade, and when he got behind the wheel, she studied him from the corner of her eye. "Nice ride."

He watched her for a minute. "Wow. No comment on overcompensating for something. You must like me."

"I didn't say it. That doesn't mean I wasn't thinking it."

Madden put the car in gear and pulled out of the parking lot. "Ooo, ouch. And here I thought Reese warned us away to protect *you*."

Hold on. "Reese warned you away from me? When? Who else?"

"Uh, everyone in the organization with man parts. He spread the word when you first started."

Fire flared in her face, and she could feel her heartbeat all over her body. *I'll kill him.* So it wasn't just a strange dry spell or even her own effort to put out the back-off vibe. For the past year, not one single man in the building had so much as asked for her number. Because her big brother warned them away.

"Can you blink or something? Just a sign that you're not stroking out?"

She blinked—hard—then worked at unclenching her fists. "He hasn't done that since I was fifteen."

Madden glanced at her and reached over like he might hold her hand, but apparently thought better of it and let his arm drop to his side. "It is kind of caveman but he's just looking out for you."

"No. You were right the first time. He was afraid I'd date around, crush some egos, and make a mess at work." She wanted to be mad, but the worst part was, she couldn't blame him. The old Saralynn would have done that. But when Jacey hired her full-time, it was like the whole world shifted. Or at least her perception of it.

"Hey. You okay?" It was his soft tone more than the words that brought her back.

"Yeah." She tried a smile.

"It would be more convincing without the clenched jaw."

"I'm okay, really. Reese's threat didn't entirely work anyway. You asked me out."

"What can I say? I'm a risk-taker." He winked at her, and the past crumbled away. It didn't matter right now. Tonight, she was the new and improved Saralynn taking a real chance on a guy. They passed a glowing sign that said "The Neon Boneyard Park" before Madden pulled into a lot just around the corner. He cut the engine and looked at her tiny purse. "So you brought a camera?"

Embarrassment crept in before she even had a chance to show it to him. "Yeah."

"You'll need to take it out now."

"I ... what is this place? What's going on?"

Excitement transformed his face to a five-year-old's. "This is where Vegas signs go to die. Normally, they only do guided tours, but they make an exception for photographers, and even that's usually a two-week waiting list, but they had a cancellation. I may have blurred the truth to get us an hour alone here, so we have to keep up the cover. Let's see your camera."

She slipped her wrist out of the looped zipper pull and tried to think of a reason not to open the purse, but he looked ready to bounce out of the car without her if she delayed much longer. She wrinkled her nose and pulled it out.

His brows furrowed, and he leaned closer. "That's a camera?"

"It's the only one I have. You said I couldn't use my phone."

"Yeah, but it's so small. And pink. And plastic. Is that a Hello Kitty sticker?"

She groaned. "Yes, okay? It was a hand-me-down from Sophie, and she got it from Shiloh. And yes, it takes thirty-five-millimeter film."

"Uh, it's okay. We just won't broadcast that to management. Maybe hold your thumb over the sticker."

She felt a pout coming on, but he leaned in and kissed her cheek, and "woe is me" went out the window.

• • •

Madden hopped out the driver's side and almost tripped on a rock and face-planted in the sand in his sprint to open Saralynn's door before she could beat him to it. Her rewarding smile was so worth it. Even dressed down she still looked out of his league. He led the way into the main building shaped sort of like the Sydney Opera House and handed their tickets to the lady behind the front desk.

"You're the photographers?"

He nodded and held up a pretty impressive camera with a big zoom lens. Saralynn raised her little, pink rectangle, but only for a second. Desk lady narrowed her eyes and pursed her lips but nodded and waved toward the back door leading into the park.

Once they stepped into the cool night air alone, he let his shoulders hunch forward. "Man. I thought she was going to ask for fingerprints and dental casts."

Saralynn glided down the few steps onto the dust path and turned in a slow circle, her head tilted back to take in the massive signs all lit up or backlit in different colors. "Whoa."

"I know, right?"

"How did I not know about this place?"

"It's not one of the city's main attractions, but it should be." He shuffled down then took a few backward steps into the maze but kept watching her take it all in.

"This is amazing." It felt pretty great to claim credit for the awe on her face.

"Come on." He held out his arm. It wasn't flattering when she stared at it like an alien tentacle, but she looped her arm around and held on tentatively. Baby steps. "So what do you think?"

"I love it. It feels like an abandoned carnival. Spooky but really cool."

"That's the vibe I get, too. Especially at night. Kinda romantic though, huh?"

She glanced at him sideways and didn't say anything, but that smile was enough. "So you learned all about me on the last shared evening."

"You wanted to say date."

"Did not." Her tongue flashed at him, and he resisted pulling her in for a kiss.

"My mistake."

"Anyway, it's my turn. If we're going to get to know each other, we really have to put it all out there and open up. Do you agree?"

His stomach sank, but at the same time, hope expanded in his chest. "Sure. Okay."

"You seem like a pretty smart guy. How did you … I mean, what happened that … "

"I became a gambling addict?"

She glanced up at him almost shyly and nodded.

So, no easing into the shallow end. And here he'd thought he'd romance her until he could gloss over his past between flower bouquets and imported chocolates. He should have known better. Saralynn shared no other traits with women he'd dated before. This was a new frontier, and how could he deny the pretty trailblazer on his arm? Not that that made it any easier.

"I was always good with numbers, and our dad raised us to be competitive. To win every contest, and if something wasn't a contest, to turn it into one. Combine that with a decent bank account at twenty-one, and, well … I got sucked into gambling. Several twelve-step programs helped me see that was because I wanted my old man's attention, which I always kind of knew but never consciously thought about."

She nodded as they walked, clearly listening, but keeping her gaze on the glowing signs. Whether she did it on purpose to make him more comfortable while he bared his soul or he just wasn't that interesting, it was hard to tell. Either way, gratefulness lifted the weight of embarrassment. Her small fingers tightened on his forearm, and the simple reassurance did more than she could know. "I could see that. As the baby girl of my family, I probably got spoiled, but I was also a surprise. My siblings let me know it. I think I might have tried harder to stand out and be as perfect as I could to make up for being the extra."

"Trust me. You are nobody's afterthought."

Her ear-to-ear smile took away any of his remaining insecurity. She touched her temple to his shoulder. "Tell me about your sister."

"Jace was always the overachiever, the focused one. I'd get her teachers in high school, and without fail, they'd say, 'You're Jacquelyn's brother. You have a lot to live up to.' As if I didn't know. I bet they still use her term papers as examples. But she worked hard at everything she did, including raising me."

"Raising you? Your parents weren't involved?"

A pang of sadness hit him in the gut even though he didn't really remember his mother. You didn't have to remember someone to miss them. "Our mom died when I was four. We have albums up until that time, but I don't have many memories of her. And Dad, after she died, threw himself into his work. We had nannies, but Jace looked out for me. Read to me, made sure I did my homework. Gave me advice about girls, taught me to drive. I have to give her a lot of credit for that one. I was a Formula One racer right out of the gate."

"That does not surprise me."

"Hey." He nudged her ribs with his elbow, which earned him a hip bump. "So Jace went away to college, I stayed local and made some bad choices. Followed the old man around and tried to impress him, but my mistakes overshadowed my best intentions. When he left the team to Jacey, I was disappointed, but she deserved it."

Saralynn stopped and pulled out her toy camera to take a few pictures of a Stardust sign with red-orange letters and a purple background. "Are you happy as assistant GM?"

"It's a good job. I get to be involved with the team, but the responsibility isn't overwhelming. In fact … " He'd been doing less and less lately, and not by choice. It had started just after the gambling rumor.

"In fact?" She looked over her shoulder at him.

It wouldn't help to speculate with her. Not to mention it was pretty emasculating to think his sister and brother-in-law were secretly benching him and pretending that everything was business as usual. Unease settled just below the surface, but he pushed it out of his mind for the moment. "I could probably do more. Lighten some of the load around the office." He'd just have to convince Jacey.

"That's very proactive." Saralynn returned to his arm and led the way down the winding path, occasionally kicking a piece of old glass out of the way with the toe of her sneaker. "I think that's enough serious stuff for tonight, how 'bout you?"

"Agreed."

"Oh! Cool!" She skipped over to a sign that said "Sin" and posed sideways at the end of it, arms crossed under her chest. "Take my picture?"

"Absolutely." He adjusted the settings on his camera and framed it up before taking the shot, though it was hard to pay attention to anything except the sexy woman dominating the screen. "Okay, good."

She jogged back, skidded to a stop pressed against his side, and leaned in to check it out. "I love it. Can we use this promotionally? I mean just a picture of the sign. It'd be a great way to tie the team in to the community."

Her cotton candy scent filled his head and delayed his answer. "Uh, yeah. The 'professional package' tickets let us do whatever we want with the pictures we take tonight."

"Excellent. Do you mind taking one more of the sign? I promise the next shot won't be team-related." Mischief sparked in her dark eyes and sped up his pulse.

"Ohh-kay." He took the picture, and then she took the camera. "Hey."

She grinned and pointed to a wedding chapel sign. "This one's for fun. Stand there."

Contagious excitement mixed with curiosity spurred him to follow her directions while she fidgeted with the camera buttons then set it at eye level on a sign aimed at him. "Okay, ready?"

"Ready for—"

Before he could finish, she jogged over, grabbed him by the hands, and pulled him flush against her for a searing kiss. A light flashed, and for all he knew, it was every bulb in the park exploding from the sheer power of their connection. And then it didn't matter that she'd only done it for the picture because the kiss took on a life of its own.

Her hands left his and explored his back, holding him closer, which made his jeans a little tighter. She teased his bottom lip with her tongue, and he invited her in with a soft groan. One of her legs hooked around his thigh, and he grabbed it to steady her while his free arm circled her lower back for maximum contact.

Her fingers delved into his hair, and the kiss turned hungry, desperate. Nothing else existed.

Finally, she pulled back, gasping, and put a foot of space between them, though she still held onto his forearms and swayed a bit. "Holy wow."

He sucked air and willed blood back to his brain. "Yeah." Never in his life had he wanted someone so much, but it clearly wasn't the place. Or the time. He didn't want to rush her.

"So, to be continued?" She licked her lips and straightened her dress, and he tried to form a coherent thought.

Pursuing this, whatever it was or might be, could blow up in his face. If things didn't work out, aside from the ramifications at work, there was a personal risk. If Jacey thought he was irresponsible, he might not get to know his niece or nephew. He didn't gamble anymore. But something about Saralynn made him want to roll the dice.

"Yes, please."

Chapter Ten

She's not avoiding me. Whether that was denial or a declaration, Madden didn't know. He'd called Jacey on Sunday to see if they could meet up for lunch, but she said she had plans with Carter. That could have been true, except he knew her tells. The girl could not lie well to save her life. And now here he stood, staring at the arena's basement elevator, trying to believe it wasn't a big deal. While he was considerably better at stretching the truth than his sister, he couldn't lie to himself.

The strong impulse to play hooky stilled his hand from pushing the button, but he fought it and won. It was only 8 a.m., an hour before the offices officially opened, but Jacey would be here. She always was. No better time for a most likely heartbreaking chat.

The elevator seemed to go extra slow, and the walls seemed extra close. *Is it hot in here?* He tugged at the neck of his T-shirt and was about to slip the blazer off his shoulders when the doors opened and a gust of cool air conditioning hit him, drying the sweat on his neck and making him feel clammy. Swallowing was a lost cause, just a dry click. But the light was on in the office at the end of the hall, and against his better judgment, his feet kept moving.

He knocked once then stepped inside. Jacey looked up, surprised. She tried to cover it with a smile, but it didn't quite work. "Hey, Madden."

Oh boy. If she wasn't calling him Maddie, it had to be bad. His stomach turned upside down, and he almost fell into the chair opposite her desk. "Hey. Thought I'd come in early so I could talk to you."

She shuffled papers around her desk, organized her pens. Normal Jacey behavior but with a nervous edge. "What's on your mind?"

He could still back out. He didn't have to ask the questions he was pretty sure he didn't want answers to. But he needed them. "Lately, Carter's been taking meetings for me. It's his right as GM, but for the last year, I've been talking to player agents and other teams on my own, no problem. And I noticed it started right after the gambling rumor. Jace … do you not trust me?" Those last words came out an almost-whisper and hurt like barbed wire being pulled out of his throat.

She wouldn't meet his eyes, just stared at her ink blotter, hands flat on her desk. That hesitation choked him up, and he bit the inside of his cheek hard to hold back the tears that wanted to surface. Finally, Jacey cleared her throat. "I want to trust you. Carter, too. He took those meetings because I asked him to. It's an important time for the team, shaping up for next season, and I just wanted to make sure—"

"I wouldn't go on a bender and come in drunk?"

Her eyes flared at him and held regret and sadness but also a hint of defiance. "You came in hung over the day after the bachelor party."

"It was a *bachelor party*. Maybe I had a few more drinks than the other guys, but I'd just seen my ex saying 'I do' to someone else. Don't I get any slack?"

She almost said something but didn't. Didn't have to. *You've gotten all the slack I can give* was plain on her face. It broke his heart all over again.

"You can count on me, Jace. I know you couldn't before, but you can now. I didn't gamble that night. I haven't gambled since … well, you know. It's a choice every day, but I make it because you mean too much to me. So does this team. I swear."

Tears slid down her cheeks, and she wiped them away with a small sniffle, but she nodded. The fist of tension in his gut unclenched just a little. She grabbed a tissue and dabbed at her face. "I love you, Maddie. Always have, always will. And I love this team, too. I'd like you and Carter to take the remaining meetings together today and tomorrow. Trade deadline's on Wednesday, so it's crunch time."

That was fair. The bigger the player names, the closer to the deadline their decisions ran. It made sense for Carter to be in those meetings. At least she wasn't cutting him out entirely. "Okay, boss."

That got a smile out of her even if it also triggered an eye roll.

"Well, I'll just get out of your hair then. And Jace? I love you, too."

The tears threatened again. She balled the tissue in her hand and nodded with a watery smile. He winked and turned heel before he could lose it. His palm was so sweaty, it almost slid off the doorknob, but he slipped out and took a deep breath.

People began to filter into their offices, but none seemed to notice him, or they pretended not to. The scent of coffee lured him to Saralynn's door. She had the radio on quietly and was dancing around as she filed papers and scribbled on neon Post-it notes that she stuck on the cabinet. He knocked lightly on the slightly open door.

• • •

She spun around with a gasp, hands pressed to her chest. When she saw it was Madden, she relaxed. When she saw his entertained grin, she hopped forward to smack his arm. "Don't *do* that!"

He laughed, and she smacked him again. He rubbed it with an exaggerated pout. "Oww. Sorry. Didn't mean to scare you. Okay, maybe a little."

She raised her hand again, but he caught her wrist and kissed the inside of it. Her pulse shot up, and her whole body flushed. She wanted to lean into him and pick up where they left off Saturday night. Instead, she yanked her hand away and closed her door behind him. "Are you out of your mind?"

"No." He tilted his head side to side. "Pretty sure it's still there."

A little giggle bubbled up in her throat, but she held it back. "Can I do something for you?"

His blue eyes darkened, and he curled an arm around her waist, pulling her close for a devilishly sweet kiss. So sweet, it was a whole minute before she remembered where they were. She put a hand to his chest and pushed him back a step but couldn't bring herself to remove her hand right away. When she did, she shook it to relieve the sensation of his hard, warm muscle. Though her blinds were closed and no one could possibly overhear, she whispered, "We can't do that here!"

He pecked her cheek lightning quick then fell into a chair. She blinked, then cleared off the section of her desk facing him and sat on it. For the first time, she really looked at him. His eyes were a little red, but not bloodshot. More like he'd just been crying. Her chest felt tight, and she reached out and brushed her fingers along the back of his hand. "Hey. What happened?"

He met her gaze but didn't answer right away. She knew that look. He was searching for an excuse, debating what to tell her. She knew because she imagined she'd looked just like that when previous guys had asked her what she was thinking and "I'm so bored" wasn't an option.

But then his features softened, and he looked at his lap. "I talked to Jace. She was having Carter take meetings for me because she questioned my judgment after last week. We worked it out though. We're good now. I think."

The pain rolled off him so tangibly, it hurt her, too. She lifted his chin and held his gaze. "If you're not, you will be."

The gratefulness in his face could have taken out her knees if she weren't already sitting. He caught her hand and kissed her palm. "Thanks."

She nodded and looked away. It was too much, the way he looked right into her. Her gaze landed on the duffle bag by the bookcase at the same time his did. *Oops.* She looked away and was about to change the subject, but it was too late.

"What's that?"

"Hmm? Nothing, just my gym bag."

"A gym bag, but what's … " He pushed out of the chair and knelt by the duffle before she could get to it. He pulled out a glittery tank top that said "Lady Sinners" in white rhinestones. "No. Way."

"It's not like I'm one of them or anything. I just join in on practices."

"Then why do you have this?" He smiled and held it up.

His teasing was way better than almost crying, so she didn't hit him. She snatched the tank top away. "I don't have time to work out, okay? I live here. And by that, I mean there's a sleeping bag under my desk, and sometimes I don't leave for days."

He gave her a skeptical look and leaned around her desk. His eyebrows went up before the doubt returned. "If you sleep here, where do you shower?"

"The locker room."

The surprise on his face was almost worth this humiliating confession.

"The guys aren't there. I sneak down after they leave. It's surprisingly luxe, but I still wear sandals. It's called athlete's foot for a reason. I keep a makeup bag in my desk. It's not like I do it all the time. Usually just when there are back-to-back games and I have a lot to get done."

He just stared at her for a solid five seconds, then blinked and refocused on the glittery tank in her hand. "So you can't get to the gym a lot."

"Yeah, so Allie was telling me how she—how dance could be a good workout." Oh God, they'd been sisters for just over a week, and Saralynn had almost spilled a secret. Already. "I talk to our dance team a lot because they do so many promotions, and Miranda invited me to a practice. Turns out it's a *really* good workout. And fun. You're not gonna tell on me, are you? I'd never hear the end of it from my brother, and I'm guessing your sister wouldn't be thrilled."

"Reese, I get. I don't think Jace would care. But no. How could I? You know all my secrets. And I like you."

She'd been hearing those words since she was ten, and they usually did something for her ego, but not this time. This was so much better. When Madden said it, he didn't just mean he thought she was pretty. She wasn't blind. The man did his share of checking her out. But he also listened. He cared. And that meant more than all of the starry-eyed lemmings she'd accrued over the years. "I should know better, but I like you, too."

Now his grin was back to full strength, dimples and all. "That's the nicest thing anyone's ever said to me."

"You know, I believe that."

Playful shock filled his eyes and dropped his mouth open.

She laughed and snapped him with the tank top as if it were a locker room towel before putting it back in her bag. "I'm guessing you'll be in meetings tomorrow and early Wednesday morning right up until trades are announced. I'm going to dance practice at seven that night, but it wraps up by eight. I could meet you for a drink after. The Artisan Lounge is reporter-free, kind of out of the way, and not usually crowded. Low lighting. What do you say?"

"I say you had me at reporter-free."

Chapter Eleven

Madden leaned his head back and un-clicked his seatbelt as the garage door closed behind him. Fourteen hours at the office and they'd made five deals. Not that he had a lot to do with it. He sat there for decoration while Carter did most of the talking on conference calls. It went beyond a pride thing. It felt genuinely awful when the people who meant the most in the world to you didn't think you could do your job. Still, doing anything for fourteen hours was exhausting, even being an ineffective statue.

Sleeping in the car sounded like a viable option. It would save time in the morning when he had to be back at zero dark thirty to stand around like a placeholder. He'd thought hard about asking to share Saralynn's sleeping bag, but even she cut out around six. Plus, it wouldn't help popular opinion about him to be caught office-camping with the head of PR.

The door leading into the house opened, and Cole stood there, backlit by the chandelier in the hallway. Having a roommate wasn't always convenient, but the kid meant well. And it was probably better than sulking in the dark mansion alone like Batman, one superhero he no longer wanted to emulate. Batman might always get the girl, but he always lost her, too. *Hopefully, those days are behind me.*

He slid out of the car and bumped shoulders with Cole on the way inside. "Hey, Robin."

"Huh?"

"Nothin'. You want pizza?"

"Ahead of you. It's on the kitchen counter."

"Boy Wonder, you earn your keep."

"Oh, now I get it. Hey, why am I the sidekick?" Cole trailed him into the kitchen and took one of the stools at the island counter.

Madden sat on another and plucked a piece of pepperoni pizza from the open box. "Because you look better in tights."

"Fuck off." He laughed. "So what's the word? Who's staying, who's going? I know I'm not, but I'm curious."

Madden took a big bite, eating half of it in one mouthful, and wiped the grease on his chin with the back of his hand. "You're *never* leaving as far as management's concerned. We'll trade every last player for schmoes who will take a salary cut if it means giving the rest to you."

Cole shook his head. "You know that's not me. I like playing in Vegas. I was drafted here, and I've already won two Cups. I'm not going anywhere."

"If you put that in writing, my sister will name her firstborn after you."

"Yeah, right. Come on. Who got the ax?"

Madden picked another piece of pizza, bit off the end, and sighed. "Scotty."

"Shit, are you serious?"

He nodded. That one hadn't been easy. Scotty had a few pretty good seasons, and a couple teams had been interested in him. "He's going to Tampa."

"So who'd we get?"

"Filipelli."

"Jesus, that's incredible. I mean, I love Scotty, but Filly's a legend. Why don't you look like you just won the lottery?"

Because I didn't have anything to do with it. That was selfish, though, and the kid wouldn't understand. Dylan Cole only ever thought about the good of the team. That's what made him the best captain and a great human being. At the moment, it also made him a lousy confidant. "No, I'm happy. It's a huge score, and he'll add a lot of depth. I'm just tired, dude."

"I get that. Any other big news?"

No was on the tip of his tongue, but he paused. Cole might be only twenty-two, but he was far from typical of the age. All the guys on the team confided in him because he kept secrets and because he gave surprisingly helpful advice. Just in the short time they'd been roommates, he'd proven his worth a hundred times over. Sharing the news about Jacey's pregnancy wasn't an option. That was her announcement to make. More than that, it was dirty laundry he didn't want to air. The Saralynn thing was a different story. It would feel good to tell someone.

"This is about a girl, isn't it? Tell me you're not messing with the married chick after you crashed her wedding."

"Hell no. I learned that lesson. Finally."

"All right, so how bad can it be?"

Madden winced. "First you have to swear not to tell anyone. I mean it. Especially no one on the team."

Cole got that light bulb look with big eyes and a loose jaw. "Holy shit, it's Saralynn. Reese will *kill* you." So much for baby Yoda.

"He would if he knew. But he won't. Got it?" That scenario flashed through his mind, and he rubbed the back of his neck. He might be the same height as Reese, but the guy was strong and fast. And with the big brother motivation going, there was no telling what kind of damage the goalie could do.

"I won't say anything, but he's gonna find out. Eventually. Unless this is just a fling or something."

"It's not a fling." The words came out sure and reflexive, but truthfully, he didn't know what it was. It didn't seem like a fling. That's not what he wanted, but he couldn't read Saralynn's mind. Usually, he could get a pretty good feel for a woman's intentions, but this one was a mystery.

"All right. So unless you don't invite him to the wedding, Reese is gonna find out."

"Yeah, but like you said, eventually. We're taking things slow, getting to know each other. We want to see if there's something there worth setting off Mount Saint Reese."

Cole chugged some water and worked on his own piece of pizza. "Well, you must really like her to even risk it."

That was true. He didn't bother adding that he rarely met a risk he didn't take. The stakes to be with Saralynn were high, but that wasn't the main appeal. At least, he didn't think so. She intrigued him. Kept him guessing. At the same time, even if it didn't make perfect sense, he felt safe with her. A weird thought and one that had never occurred to him with anyone else, but there it was. "She's something."

"I gotta hand it to you, man. She's intimidatingly pretty. Even before Reese issued his threat to everyone in the building with a Y chromosome, I was too scared to talk to her. And then what he said about how she ate men for breakfast and spit out their bones, that was enough for me."

Madden barked a laugh. "Yeah. She's tough; I'll say that. But she's not as bad as Reese said. She's trying to be the best version of herself, and I can relate to that."

Cole regarded him quietly for a minute, then nodded. "Good for both of you. I hope it works out. Your sister know?"

He directed his gaze to the pizza box.

The kid whistled low. "Good luck with that."

"Thanks. I open up to you, and that's the best you got?"

"I'm sorry, dude, but this just got a lot more complicated. Is there a policy about dating a co-worker?"

"That would be a little hypocritical, don't you think? Seeing as Jace *married* the last guy who had your job. There's no formal rule, but that doesn't mean she wouldn't fire me. She's put up with too much of my shit for too long. If things went bad with Saralynn

... I guess I couldn't blame Jace." That didn't make it hurt any less. And if it came to leaving the team, what would their personal relationship be like? Over the past two years, they'd gotten closer than they'd ever been. A few forgotten poker chips in his pocket and they were back at square one, only now he had twice as much to lose. Uncle Madden had a nice ring to it. He didn't want to give that up.

"Hey. It'll be okay with you and Jacey. Even watching from the sidelines, it's easy to see how much you mean to each other. It'll take a lot more than a potentially bombed romantic relationship to ruin it."

"Thanks for the 'potentially.'"

"S'what I'm here for. So how long have you and Baby Reese been testing the waters?"

"Gah. Please don't call her that. I really don't want to picture his ugly mug every time I kiss her. And we've been seeing each other since just after the wedding." Only a week and a half, but he felt like he'd known her forever.

"Have you, uh—"

"No. Even *my* definition of slow is slower than that." Granted, that was a relatively new development, but times changed. People, too.

"All right, all right. When do you see her next?"

"Tomorrow night. She wants to meet me for drinks at the Artisan Lounge."

"Never been there. And I think I've hit all the well-known spots in Vegas, so it should be low-key."

"I haven't either, but that's what Saralynn said. It's not like we can go to Surrender, the Sinners' version of Cheers."

"Not unless you want to surrender your life to Shane Reese. Now that I know, you could always bring her here. I could go out for the night."

"Thanks. I'll see how she feels about it." It made sense, but she'd been nervous alone with him in the owner's box. Hell, he'd been nervous. And he'd meant what he said. He didn't want to pressure her or rush things. "What about you? How are things with Tricia?"

"Great, I think. She's been coming to every home game, and we go out when we both have the night off. I really like her."

"Good for you, man. You deserve it." And he did. It couldn't be easy being the poster boy for an entire sport while he was so young, but Cole pulled it off and magically remained his humble, genuine self. "Want to hit up the Xbox for a while? I need to shoot things before I go to bed."

"I hear that."

Chapter Twelve

"We really don't know if we can let him go for that much." How many times had someone said those words in the last hour? The Tampa Bay Lightning GM didn't want to give up one of his star defensemen. That was the real issue. No matter that Tampa couldn't afford to keep him. Madden took a slow breath and longed for the days of conference phone calls instead of video chats. No one could hear you roll your eyes or play dead. Time to up the ante.

"We understand that, sir. What if we threw in a prospect or two?" He'd offer a draft pick, but the Sinners had won the Cup back to back the last two years, so they got last pick in the draft, which wouldn't mean much. *Shit.* He glanced at Carter, who nodded in approval. Madden hadn't meant to make the offer out of turn, but it was the only card they had left to play, and thankfully his brother-in-law knew that. It sucked having to ask permission to do his job.

"Well ... I think we could make that work."

Thank you, Jesus.

"I'm glad to hear that. Let's talk details." Carter finished the deal, going through the Sinners' list of prospects and picking midrange players, which was fair. Madden sat back and stared at the screen without seeing it anymore. He'd rolled into the arena at four in the morning because doing business with the East Coast meant working with their time zone, and every minute counted today. It was now ten to 7 p.m. After a fifteen-hour day, all he really wanted to do was go home and face-plant on the couch. Only one person could convince him to do otherwise, and she'd be getting ready to dance with the Lady Sinners right about now.

A loud click yanked him back to the moment. Carter closed his eyes and slid a hand through his hair. Madden smiled. "Bet you're wishing for the days when you were the one being traded."

"You have no idea. But I love this job, and if I can't play, it's the second best thing. I can keep helping my team from the other side of the ice. Just still transitioning I guess."

"I don't envy you, man."

Carter went quiet and studied him for an uncomfortable minute. Finally, he cleared his throat and focused on the dark video screen. "I'm sorry about last week. Shadowing you, sitting in on your meetings. I never thought you slipped up. Okay, you came in a little under the weather the day after the bachelor party, but we all did to some extent. It's just harder for Jacey, you know?"

Madden did know. Too well. And while it lifted some weight knowing his brother-in-law hadn't lost faith in him, it hurt even more knowing how completely his sister had lost hope. Every time he'd messed up before, the one thing that got him through was Jacey's unwavering presence and support. He'd had her in his corner no matter what, and that was invaluable. It's what helped him stop gambling for good. And now, when he finally was fixing his life, the ghosts of past mistakes were winning after all. "I know. It's not her fault."

"You two have a long history, and I don't know it all, but I do know how much she loves you. It's just recently she's been … " Carter shook his head.

"Pregnant. Congratulations, by the way."

"She told you. Good. And thanks. It's a lot to wrap my head around, but I'm excited. I know it's not my place to get in the middle, but for what it's worth, I see you're trying. Just stay out of trouble, and this'll all blow over."

"Thanks. That's the plan. And it's okay. Really. If Jacey didn't double-cover all her bases, she wouldn't be my sister. It's fine." Because what alternative was there?

"All right, man. It's been a long day. What do you say we head out?"

"Yeah. I'll be right behind you. I just want to clean some of the debris off my desk from the past few days."

Carter patted his shoulder in passing.

Madden waited until he heard the elevator close at the end of the hall then collected his things and checked his watch. He could swing by the press box and catch a few minutes of dance practice down on the ice or go home for a shower and shave. Personal hygiene won out but just barely. Watching Saralynn dance had definite appeal but not as much as the opportunity to kiss her later, and that wouldn't happen without some sprucing up. In a little over an hour, he'd have her all to himself. Suddenly, the day didn't seem so bad.

• • •

"Woo! Good practice!" Saralynn scrubbed her wristband across her forehead and grabbed her water bottle from the players' bench. Amazing how much you could sweat on ice wearing so little. She high-fived a few girls as they headed out but hung back and let everyone else leave first. After the last goodbye, she checked that the coast was clear before slipping into the locker room. The showers with the heated tile flooring were calling her name.

"Sare?"

That wasn't the tiles. That was her brother. Several years into adulthood, and his way of questioning and accusing at the same time still spiked her blood pressure. She faced him and tried for an innocent look, but that was hard with her Lady Sinners tank top glittering under the locker room fluorescents. "Hey, bro."

"Tell me you're not auditioning for the dance team." He scrubbed his head with a towel, having apparently finished late in the workout room.

"I'm not auditioning for the dance team. I'm just dancing with them."

He blinked, and she could tell he was two seconds from snarking, "What's the difference?"

"Not at games. Just practices. Since I practically live in the arena, it made sense. Plus it's way more fun than running on a treadmill. And I can't tell you how glad I am that I didn't hit the showers five minutes earlier."

Her brother made a face, then pressed the heels of his palms into his eye sockets. "Ahhh, stop talking."

"Gladly. I'm running late."

"For what?"

Shit. "A date. Don't you have a wife to get home to?"

"A date with who?"

She fought back a shriek rising in her throat. Ohhh, she wanted to chew him out for threatening all the men in a three-mile radius so they wouldn't ask her out. He had no right. But if she did that, he'd want to know who told, and even though he wouldn't get the answer from her, he'd strong-arm everyone in the building until someone squealed. From there, it was a short leap to figuring out she was seeing Madden, and then her brother would blow a gasket. She un-balled her fists. "Guy I met at the radio station for the Sinners segment. Inquisition over? It takes a while to get from sweaty mess to datable, so if you don't mind … "

He eyed her warily for a minute, then shook his head and tossed his duffle bag over his shoulder. "Be safe. And make sure this radio guy knows you have an older brother with a goalie stick."

She rolled her eyes at his back as he left then threw a few spastic punches into empty air when the door closed. Sufficiently drained of pent rage, she hit the showers.

Chapter Thirteen

Date night:

The Artisan Lounge was nearly empty at just after nine on a Wednesday night. Perfect. Saralynn flipped her hair back over her shoulders and put a little sway in her step to make her entrance when she saw Madden watching from a leather sofa in the back. Sure, she could have gone for casual, but the devil on her shoulder seemed to have dibs on the megaphone when it came to this man. She couldn't resist a slinky black dress that hit mid-thigh or her favorite pair of Louboutin simple heels. Even though "simple" for Louboutin meant four inches. It was all worth the transparent desire and admiration on Madden's face.

He was looking perfectly jumpable himself in gray suit pants and a white, button-down shirt with the sleeves rolled to his elbows. "Other than the wedding, I think this is the first time I've ever seen you out of jeans."

His tired eyes sparked, and that heart-stopping grin made a grand appearance. "You can see me out of these, too, if you want." Playful, but not entirely kidding if the underlying current of heat was any indicator.

Yes, please. She tingled from head to toe, and lust pooled warm in her belly, but she tried for a nonchalant smirk. "Nice. And thank you." She nodded to the pink cosmo sitting on the coffee table next to his ... Scotch? Must have been a rough day.

"My pleasure. Have a seat. I don't bite, but I make no promises about ear nibbling."

She dropped down next to him, crossing her legs. "You are such a dork. You realize your lines wouldn't be half as effective if you weren't so ... "

"Devastatingly handsome?"

Yes. "Adorable."

"Damn. You gonna tell me I have a nice personality next? 'Cause I don't think I could take that today."

"That bad, huh?" She angled to face him and picked up her drink, taking a fortifying sip. Storms lurked under his smooth surface, and she wanted to steel her sails.

"It was a long day. We went back and forth with Tampa for hours but finally picked up Yaroslav."

"That's a good thing."

"It is."

"Someone should tell your face."

He cracked a smile and gave her a sideways glance. "Also, Carter let me know he's on my side and doesn't doubt my ability to do my job."

"That's another good thing."

"It would be if it didn't mean all of the doubt is coming from my sister."

She didn't have a response for that. She could tell him again that everything would work out. Jacey would get past the emotional roadblocks. But she didn't want to discount how badly he felt at the moment. Not sure what else to do, she set her drink back down then slowly shifted to lean her cheek on his shoulder. It was awkward at first, and he glanced down at her curiously.

"New at this, huh?"

She scrunched her face and swatted his chest. "I'm trying to comfort you here. I'm doing my best."

His features softened, and the clouds in his eyes started to subside. "You're doing great."

That connection snared her, and she couldn't look away. He dipped in and brushed his whisper-soft lips over hers, tentative. Even after their make-out session in the Boneyard, he still wasn't sure she wanted him. Silly man. She cupped his jaw with one hand and pulled him closer, deepening the kiss. Physical want consumed her, but something else, too.

She felt something for this man. Something potentially very scary but not in a horror movie kind of way. It wasn't like she thought she'd wake up to him standing over her with a chainsaw some night. No, scary in a thrilling sense, like jumping off the Stratosphere. That incredible rush coupled with the assurance of knowing you were safe. Something she'd never thought about or wanted. Until now.

His fingertips brushed a strand of her hair behind her ear, so gentle, like he thought he might break her. Or he was afraid she might break him. Both were sweet and kind of funny. She leaned back just a centimeter so they were nose to nose and smiled. "New at this, huh?"

The look in his half-lidded eyes said *challenge accepted*, and he dove back in, one hand cupping the back of her head and the other curling around her waist and pulling her flush against him. His tongue parted her lips and found her own, and she hung on for dear life. When he traced circles on the small of her back, she forgot her own name. It took every ounce of restraint not to climb him like a jungle gym. They were in a bar after all.

She pushed away with a gasp, smoothed her hair, and tugged down the hem of her dress. "Okay. So you've had some practice."

Was that a blush? Hard for a ginger to hide it. He really was painfully cute. Madden cleared his throat and shrugged. "Maybe a little. I don't usually get carried away in public. You seem to bring it out in me."

"I'll take that as a compliment."

"You absolutely should."

She pursed her lips and narrowed her eyes. "I really want to take you home with me."

"I second that motion, but I detect some indecision."

"It's just … I think I might really like you."

"That makes sense." He nodded his head then shook it.

"What I mean is, I've rushed into physical relationships before with guys I didn't care that much about. Not often. I'm not saying I was a slut, but that was almost never the right choice, and I really like you, and I think this could actually be something, and I don't want to mess it up. And I'm rambling. I never ramble, so that's proof that this is something."

He'd sat through her mini-speech with a half-smile but fought to stay serious like he was trying extra hard to follow along. When she finished and took a breath, his earnest, adoring look almost stole it away again. He wasn't the first guy to look at her like that, but this was the first time she didn't get that tiny stab of guilt for not feeling the same way. It was replaced by a touch of fear that for once she might have found something she didn't want to lose.

Madden laced his fingers through hers and squeezed. "I know what you mean. This is something, and I don't want to do anything to mess it up either. What if you come over my place, and we keep it PG? Maybe PG-13."

Easier said than done when R-rated images conga-ed through her brain every time she looked at him. "It's getting kind of late, but—wait. You live with Cole, right?"

He froze for a few seconds, then nodded slowly. "Yeah, uh, it's okay because I kind of … told him." The puppy-waiting-to-be-hit-by-a-newspaper expression was the only thing that saved him. That and the fact that she hadn't entirely kept quiet, either.

"You told him? How much does he know? God, he's not going to tell my brother, is he?"

"No, no. Cole is cool. He knows we're lying low for now. He's even the one who suggested I bring you over. He offered to go out for the night when or if you ever wanted to."

"Oh … " It still didn't feel great knowing the captain of the team was aware of their relationship, but he did seem trustworthy from what she'd heard about him. "Well, in the interest of full disclosure, Allie knows."

His eyes bugged briefly. "She—okay. All right. I guess a sister-in-law slash psychiatrist is the best person to trust with something like this. But are you sure *she* won't tell your brother? Y'know, pillow talk?"

"Ummm, no. Allie won't tell him. Especially not in bed, and give me a minute to get *that* image out of my head, thank you very much. It would kind of kill the mood if my brother went tomato red and shot through the roof. Al doesn't want to deal with that, and when the time comes, she can plead ignorance."

"When the time comes. So you can see telling your brother about us?" The hopeful note in his voice struck a chord in her heart, but the mental picture of her brother losing his shit sort of rained on the moment.

"Maybe."

He seemed to know not to push anymore and nodded. "It is getting late, and we do have to work tomorrow. How about Friday? My place for a night of good, clean fun?"

"Good and clean are in Madden Vaughn's vocabulary?"

"They are for you."

Hard to say no to that.

Chapter Fourteen

Saralynn spun around in her desk chair. For circulation, not because it was a fun way to break up the day. Besides, she had only a minute before the next player came in. She'd been sitting since one in the afternoon, and it was almost five. Whose brilliant idea had it been to spice up the in-house player trading cards? Oh right. Hers. Not that it was all bad. She'd gotten a few interesting answers to the most popular questions submitted from Sinners fans. For example, Ben Collier wore neither boxers nor briefs. Holding eye contact through *that* interview had been damn near impossible, but she'd managed.

The whole day had been one long Russian roulette as she waited for Cole to appear. The impending awkwardness hung over her like a clingy storm cloud. She'd have to be professional and straight-faced in front of the guy who knew she was secretly rendezvousing with the boss's brother. Second on the trepidation list was seeing her own brother, the human polygraph. Sure, she'd kept things from him in the past, but that worked better with a few thousand miles between them.

Cole came in first. The Sinners captain eased the door closed behind him and looked around the office, glancing at her quickly then focusing on the Sinbad mascot Bobblehead on her desk. The poor guy looked more nervous than she was.

"Okay, this is silly. I know you know about Madden and me, and yes, we'd like to keep it under wraps, but there's no reason things should be weird here. I can't imagine what you might have heard from Reese. I'd like to say it's not true, but it probably is.

Or was." All cards on the table up front. Not her usual style in the past, but new leaf, new tactics.

Cole took the chair facing her desk and slumped back with a sigh. "It's good to hear that. I wasn't sure what to say or how to act. Mad's like a brother. He's a good guy. And the whole thing with Linden really messed him up."

"I know." That now-familiar ache at what that woman put him through set in. But a small part of her worried she might be no better. "Shall we get started?"

"Shoot."

"All right. First up: what scares you?" Her fingers hovered over the computer keys, and she stared at the screen. And stared. A glance at him revealed downcast eyes. "It can't be that bad. Trust me. Colly's afraid of ladybugs."

That got a smile. "Yeah? Okay, clowns. Went to a haunted house when I was five. The whole time you hear that high, insane laugh. Get to the end, think you're home free, and a clown jumps out with a chainsaw and blood dripping from his mouth. Well, fake blood, I guess."

"Jesus. Now I'm afraid of clowns. Moving on. Okay, this one's better. Guilty pleasure?"

"I don't think you should feel guilty about the things you like, but if we're going by what the guys rag on me for, I listen to Aretha Franklin before games."

"R-e-s-p-e-c-t. Don't have to defend that to me."

"It was playing in the rink before my first peewee game. Got a hat trick in the first period."

Her fingers paused over the keys, and she blinked at him. "Whoa." The whole world knew Cole was a phenom, but that was one story she'd never heard.

He shrugged and picked at the knee of his jeans.

"Boxers or briefs?"

"Uh, boxers. People really want to know this about us?"

"The fans who typically answer our surveys are women, and you bet they do. That's why the pictures on these cards will be shirtless. Are you okay with that?"

"I'm not embarrassed or anything, I just don't see what it has to do with hockey."

"Not a thing. It's more about growing the fan base and hitting an untapped market. If games are the only place these cards are available, more women will buy tickets. The dance team appeals to the male demographic. This one's for the ladies."

"Hockey's not good enough?"

Clearly, for him it was, and that shot him up another 100 points on the endearing scale. "Sadly, no. Not in a desert state. But I might be out of a job if it were. Think of it this way. The cards get them in the door; the hockey makes them come back."

The corner of his mouth quirked up. "I guess that's okay."

"Two more questions. What's your perfect date?"

"I'd want to do whatever she's passionate about. Like my girlfriend now, she's a singer. For our first date, we went to karaoke. I wanted to see her in her element, doing what she loves. That confidence is really sexy, and you know she's having a good time."

"Excellent. Last one. Describe your perfect woman."

"That's easy. She'd have to be driven, with goals of her own, but still know how to have fun. She would need to understand my busy schedule and trust that if I'm with her, I'm not with anyone else. I just want to be with someone who gets me, and there's no pretending." It was so honest. The other guys gave mostly stock answers like being nice or having a sense of humor.

"Thanks, Cole. You can send Reese in on your way out."

"No problem. Oh, and uh, I'm staying at Tricia's tomorrow night, so you don't have to worry about … anything." Annnd the awkward was back.

"Oh, okay."

He waved and slipped out the door. She had three seconds to decompress before her brother swung in and sat across from her, looking wary. "You're not dating Cole, are you?"

"*No*. I told you. A guy from the radio station. We're here to talk about you anyway."

He didn't disagree, but it wasn't over.

"Let's just get through this, and then we can both go home. First question. What scares you?"

"Nothing."

"Ummm, I call bullshit. I grew up with you, remember?"

"Okay. *Twilight*."

Or the dark. The man had slept with a nightlight at least until he left home in his early teens. But he'd never admit to that now, and she did want to get home. "Fine. Guilty pleasure?"

"Bubble baths."

"Seriously?"

"With my wife."

Gag. Oh God. The next question stuck in her throat. She cringed. "Boxers or briefs?"

"Boxer-briefs. Just enough support and—"

"Got it. That's enough." She squeezed her eyes closed as she typed the answer then moved along. "Perfect date?"

"Staying in to eat pizza, play video games, and catch some hockey on TV." His glazed eyes and satisfied smirk meant that date actually happened. Had to have been with Allie because no other woman could have known her brother so well.

"Okay. Perfect woman?"

"My wife. She knows me better than I do, she's always there when I need her, and I couldn't imagine spending my life with anyone else. She opened me up and showed me everything I didn't know I was missing."

Saralynn stopped typing halfway through his answer. The words settled deep. Madden was starting to do all those things for her. She couldn't imagine the rest of her life at the moment, but the snapshot she could see had him in it. Front and center. "That's really sweet. I couldn't have picked someone better for you. Oh wait. I did pick her."

"Still trying to take credit."

"Only when I deserve it. All right, we're done. Go home to Allie. I'll go home to my TV and a pizza."

His expression softened, and as he stood, he leaned over the desk to peck her forehead. "You really are growing up. I'm proud of you, Sare." He paused in the doorway and pointed at her. "Doesn't mean I won't background check your boyfriends."

She balled up a Post-it note and pitched it at his chest. Score! He grunted and left. Reruns of *Grey's Anatomy* might be keeping her company tonight, but tomorrow, it'd be a tall, handsome executive who wanted to cook her dinner. The image of Madden in an apron was good. The image of Madden in *just* an apron wasn't far behind. Okay. Cold shower, then call for that pizza.

Chapter Fifteen

Friday, March 7th

"You never told me you lived in the Playboy Mansion."

"There are a lot of perks to this place. Not the least of which is a custom-made pool table in the game room that we'll get to later. But you'll notice the lack of bunnies. I'm a one-rabbit kind of man." Madden shut the door behind Saralynn as she stepped into the foyer and stared up at the crystal chandelier. While she admired her view, he admired his. No heels tonight but strappy wedges that still brought her to just under his chin.

"Oh yeah? Word is, you've had your share of hares." She turned that glowing smile on him.

"But never more than one at a time."

Her eyebrows arched, and she nodded as if impressed. She tilted her head up, breathed deep through her nose, then hooked a thumb toward the kitchen. "Something smells amazing. Jeeves in there?"

"Very funny. No butler, though we do have a cleaning service that comes once a week. I do the cooking."

"You cook?"

"I'll choose not to be wounded by your shock. Go check it out."

She gave him a playfully dubious look then wandered down the hall. He almost ran into her back, she stopped so short. "You did this? All this? No catering or takeout?" She circled the island, peeking and prodding at the platters of meatloaf, red smashed potatoes, green beans, corn, and rolls.

"A little wounded now. And yeah, this is all me. Come on, it's not that fancy."

"I'm sorry; I shouldn't be surprised. Even Reese picked up some recipes from Ma and Grams. I've personally never seen them put into practice, but Allie tells me he's cooked for her. I'm counting it as a myth until I witness it myself."

"You know, Jace used to do most of the cooking, even as a preteen. When I got old enough, I took over. It was one small thing I could do to pay her back. She wasn't used to someone else taking care of her, and the look on her face when I'd make dinner was worth it."

Saralynn had that expression again. The one of pity, concern, and caring rolled together that made him regret divulging this stuff. How attractive could it be to talk about his sister on every date? He didn't mean to, but when he let his walls down, it just came out. And Saralynn was a giant wrecking ball to his normally carefully guarded fortress.

She crossed back to him and picked up his hand. "Well, this looks really good. We're talking big brownie points. I might let you beat me in pool. That's a lie. I'm totally going to kick your ass, but the dinner does mean a lot."

He laughed, and the knot of uncertainty loosened in his chest. "Big talk. Better hope you can back that up."

"Or what?"

"Or I might not let you beat me at pool."

"Bring it on. I don't need your charity. I can take you just fine without it." She wiggled her brows then spun around and filled a plate with more food than he *and* Cole could possibly eat. In a week.

"Planning on a doggy bag?"

"Huh? Oh. No, I'm just hungry. Sorry. Are you used to dating models who fill up on a few spinach leaves?"

"Uh ... " In a way. Maybe not that extreme, but most women didn't usually order much on dates. It was a refreshing change.

"No, I like a woman who eats. It's just for us, so take as much as you want."

She took a seat on one of the stools, beamed at him, and ate a forkful of meatloaf. Then her eyes closed, and she moaned, which had two effects. One, pride coursed through him for the compliment to his cooking. Two, lust coursed through him when he imaged that moan in a different setting. Saralynn licked her lips—*God, not helping*—and cut another bite with her fork. "Okay, I didn't give you enough credit. This isn't filching family recipes. This is next *Food Network Star*. You have a gift."

His face burned all the way to the tips of his ears. "It's meatloaf."

"It's a masterpiece," she said around another mouthful.

"Glad you like it." He filled a plate for himself, sat beside her, and watched her eat from the corner of his eye. She squealed and tapped her feet on the bottom rung of the stool. If she were faking the enthusiasm, she deserved an Emmy. Cole had said his cooking was good, but the average twenty-two-year-old hockey player wasn't that discerning about food. If it wasn't currently breathing, moving, or growing but at one point had been, it was fair game. "So I haven't talked to you since Wednesday night. How was the rest of your week?"

She put her fork down and took a drink from the glass of soda he'd set out. "I'm sure there are worse jobs, but interviewing hockey players—especially when the questions are personal—can get weird. Times ten when one of them is your brother. I just hope this idea sells as well as I think it will. That was yesterday. Today was the photo shoot."

"I heard some stuff about that. Twenty-something half-naked hockey players. You weren't taking the pictures, were you?"

"Are you kidding? You've seen my camera. No, I left that to a professional, but I had to be there to liaise. That's French for 'corral and hold the attention span of six-foot toddlers.' Averting their pranks is a job of its own."

"Sure you weren't sponging the sweat from their foreheads or greasing their abs?" He kept his tone light and playful, and honestly, he didn't think she'd really do anything like that, but knowing she'd been surrounded by a lot of men at their physical peaks made him twitch.

She'd been stirring her corn into her potatoes and looked up at him with a knowing grin. "You're jealous."

"Am not." Okay, that sounded lame even to him. "Maybe a little. I know it's stupid."

"It's sweet." She leaned over and kissed his cheek, her hair sweeping forward to tickle his jaw. He got a whiff of her cotton candy perfume and breathed deeper.

"You smell like dessert."

"Ah-ah. What happened to PG-13? And I hope that's not your way of telling me there's no real dessert, 'cause I just cleaned my plate."

He peered around her and did a double take. "Whoa."

"I usually eat a little slower, but everything was so awesome, it's taking all my willpower not to lick every last atom of food from the ceramic."

"Thanks. And you get to pick the rating for the night. If you're set on PG-13, there's ice cream cake in the fridge. You'll save me a piece, right?"

She stuck her tongue out at him but glided around the island to retrieve the cake then stared at it. "I can't make any promises. I'm hearing the 'Hallelujah Chorus.' Did you make this, too?"

"Dairy Queen gets the credit for that one."

"Too bad. A homemade ice cream cake just might be enough to get me to say yes to a marriage proposal one of these days."

I'll keep that in mind. Wait a minute.

"How many proposals have you had so far?"

"Four. Five." She glanced at the ceiling as if doing the mental math then nodded. "Five."

"*Five?* You're twenty-three."

She gave him a sheepish smile and shrugged. "College. Besides, I'm pretty sure one or two weren't really serious about it." She concentrated on cutting two pieces of cake as if her words were no big deal.

Five proposals. He'd only been fairly serious with two women before in his life. A naïve college crush that crumbled upon graduation, and most recently, a naïve infatuation with a reporter who turned out to be Satan herself. Then finally Saralynn, who felt more right than anyone, but what chance did he have with a past like hers?

She looked up from plating the melting cake slices and pressed her lips together. "I freaked you out."

He wanted to deny it and tried to, but the words didn't come fast enough.

"You know I'm not super proud of my past. I led guys on, and I feel terrible about it, but that's not me anymore. I'm not saying I'm ready to get married or anything, but I'm not just wasting time with you. That came out wrong. What I mean is, I used to be closed off to even the possibility of love. And I'm not now. At least not entirely."

She was so serious, smiling seemed like the wrong thing to do, but he couldn't help it. He circled the counter and slid his arms around her waist, pulling her against him at the hip. "You say you don't ramble often?"

"I would hit you, but my hands are dripping with ice cream, and that looks like an expensive shirt."

He leaned in, nudged her nose with his, then kissed her. It started slow and sweet then picked up some steam. Her arms went around his neck as she swayed into him. A few cold drops hit the back of his neck, and he jerked back before remembering the ice cream on her fingers.

"Guess we should eat it before it's soup." She nodded toward the plates, where the icing was sliding off the cake.

Words eluded him. His brain was still stuck on the possibilities born from that kiss, so he bobbed his head a few times to offer some form of response. Her smile let him know she enjoyed the effect she had, and she proceeded to lick her hands clean with innocence in her big, doe eyes. A small, strangled sound came from his throat. "You're doing this on purpose."

"Doing what?" She blinked at him, fanning long, dark lashes before diving into her slice of half-melted cake. The red icing smeared across her lips, and she looked a little like a hyena devouring a fallen gazelle as she inhaled the dessert. It took some of the edge off, and he laughed. One second unbelievably sexy and the next a relatable goofball. That seemed like good relationship material.

While he polished off his own slice, she dabbed at her mouth with a napkin but didn't quite get it all. "You missed a little ... "

She tried again to no avail. He reached over and brushed the corner of her mouth, getting the last of the icing, but before he could pull back, she caught his thumb between her lips and the tip of her tongue flicked against it.

He released a slow breath. "You're killing me here."

He wasn't mistaking the desire reflected in her eyes, but she took a step back. "Sorry. Old habits. I want you, and I do see that happening. Just probably shouldn't be tonight."

She was right. His brain knew that, but it was having a little trouble getting a word in when all blood flow was directed south at the moment. He wanted her like he'd never wanted anyone in his life. Waiting would make it all the more intense. Hadn't he promised her a night of good, clean fun? Shower sex came to mind, but that was a loose interpretation, and even his hormone-riddled mind comprehended that. "In that case, I think we need a distraction. I believe someone threatened to beat me in pool."

"Wasn't a threat. It was a promise." Her smile was as sweet as her perfume.

"Then let's go."

• • •

After five games, he'd bowed deeply and admitted defeat, but Saralynn had a sneaking suspicion he'd let her win the last two. Normally she'd object, but it didn't feel like he was patronizing her. More like he enjoyed watching her victory dance. That was fair because she enjoyed watching him bend over to line up a shot. Plus, how many guys could put away their own egos, throw a game, and not rub it in all because they wanted their date to have fun? Not many, in her experience.

She hung her stick on the rack. "So what's next? A movie in the living room? That was the cavern to the left of the foyer, right? Wish we'd left a trail of breadcrumbs from the kitchen to find our way back."

"Movie yes, living room no." His light eyes had that mischievous glint that made her toes curl.

"I hope you're not suggesting we watch it in your bedroom. I have willpower, but I'm not made of steel."

He grinned and held out a hand. "Come with me."

Should I or shouldn't I repeated in her head for all of two seconds before she slid her palm into his and followed along. It wasn't poor impulse control. If that had been the case, they'd have sealed the deal Wednesday night. Or an hour ago in the kitchen. This was delayed gratification. This was … not what she expected.

Instead of going upstairs, he tugged her into a dark room that had to be enormous judging from the acoustics of the echo when he closed the door. When he flipped the lights, she gasped. There was a giant movie screen that had to be just short of IMAX, with stadium seating. Granted, not as big as an actual theater, but this was *in his house.*

"I wish I could take credit, but this was all my dad."

"This is where we're watching the movie? I can see why Cole loves it here. Not that your five-star personality isn't enough on its own."

"Hah, thanks." He winked at her and moved to turn on the projector and game system.

She went up a few steps, chose the middle of a row, and eased into the most comfortable theater seat she'd ever experienced. "Did you have auditions for a roommate? How'd Cole get the gig?"

"Are you saying you'd like to kick him out and take his place?" Madden vaulted the steps in one jump and sat beside her.

"Ah ... " He wasn't serious, right? In a place this big, she'd feel like another ornament, but living in a giant playground did hold a certain appeal. So did the thought of sharing a bed with Madden.

"Relax, I was just kidding. I don't think your shoe collection would fit in here."

She jabbed his arm with her elbow, and he laughed.

"I wasn't looking for a roommate. Even when Jace lived here, we hardly saw each other, so it wasn't much different when she got married and moved in with Carter. Cole had been bunking with a guy who got traded. Not that he couldn't afford his own place. The kid could buy a small island in the South Pacific. But it's a big city, and he's kind of shy. Still only hangs out with guys on the team and Tricia when he's not at the arena. We were talking one day, and I could tell he was nervous about being on his own, so I made the offer. Turns out it is kind of nice having someone around."

"He told me you're like a brother to him. Sounds like he's been good for you, too."

"He's a good guy. I might even miss him if he moves in with Tricia, but don't tell him I said that."

"Said what?"

He leaned over the armrest and kissed her nose. No guy had ever done that to her. It was such a simple, natural gesture, so boyfriend-y, but she'd never been the boyfriend type before. Not in any genuine way. Tingles danced through her, but not the sexy kind from earlier. This was the stomach-full-of-butterflies variety, and all she could think was *I don't want to lose this.*

Chapter Sixteen

Monday, March 10th

Madden sat across from Cole in a red vinyl booth at Johnny Rockets, staring at his cheeseburger. Cole hadn't put his down and was two bites from done. The kid took a break to swallow and wiped his mouth with the back of his hand. "You okay, man?"

"Yeah, just thinking. Sorry."

Cole set what remained of his burger on the plate, fully focused. He was dependable like that, and intuitive. He always knew when okay didn't mean okay. Sometimes it was annoying, but not today. If Madden didn't talk to someone about Saralynn, he'd combust.

"I just can't stop thinking about her, you know? And it's getting harder to keep it a secret. I want to be able to go anywhere with her, whenever, and not worry about who might find out."

"I know what you mean. When I first started seeing Tricia, we laid low to save her from the press, but eventually, she came around to the idea. I know it's different with you. More people involved and more at stake."

He didn't know the half of it. "I don't want to scare her away though. I'm afraid if we go too fast, she'll bolt. And then … part of me wonders if it's even real. I've always had this habit of jumping with both feet, getting in over my head, and sorting through the fallout after everything blew up. Bets, relationships. Hell. Even my position in the organization."

"What do you mean?"

"Ah, nothing." Oversharing. Another thing he needed to work on. "Sometimes I'm stretched a little thin."

"That, I get. But it's different with Saralynn. I can tell. You weren't like this, even about Linden."

"It feels different. I guess I'm still getting used to trusting my own judgment. And Saralynn's not always easy to read. I think we're on the same page, but can you ever really know?"

"Women can be a mystery. I feel good with Tricia though. We're pretty solid. I'm even thinking of seeing how she'd feel about moving in together." The last part he said picking at his fries, paying extra attention to how he lined them up in the ketchup.

It shouldn't have, but the thought of Cole moving out left him a little hollow and ... sad. He hadn't realized how nice it was to have someone like a younger brother around to goof off or eat dinner with. A co-captain to kill zombies with before bed. "Dude, if she's into it, go for it. You seem really happy with her, and you don't get much time together with your schedule."

Cole nodded, and his throat worked like he was trying to say something, but he didn't. He just nodded again, ate another fry, and mumbled, "Thanks, man." It hadn't been easy for the kid adjusting to big city life on his own. If he could take this step, even if it made him nervous, he had to. And Madden would support it because that's what brothers did. Even unofficial ones.

Just as Madden picked up his burger, the waitress stopped by and tilted her head with a frown. "Somethin' wrong, hon?"

"Oh, no. We were just talking, and I got sidetracked. I'm about to make it disappear like Copperfield."

Sandy, according to her name tag, smiled at Cole's empty plate. "Looks like this one can multitask."

"He's gifted."

Cole flicked a wadded straw wrapper on the table, and it landed in Madden's Coke. "He shoots, he scores!"

Sandy giggled and picked up Cole's plate and silverware. "Let me just get this out of your way. Can I interest you in dessert today?"

"I'll take the Perfect Brownie Sundae."

"You got it. Anything I can get for you, sir?"

Madden winked. "I think I'm set, thanks."

Sandy smiled politely, but it wasn't the usual female reaction to his charm. Could he be losing his mojo? Not with Saralynn, and that's all that mattered. He shrugged and ate half his burger in two bites. Three more bites, and it was gone with the fries on deck.

Cole smirked. "You weren't kidding, Copperfield."

Madden picked the wrapper out of his drink and sipped through the straw. "I'd answer you, but it would only slow me down."

"Right. Well after you finish, do you think you'll ask Saralynn to move in with you?"

That one caught him off guard. He'd joked about it the night before but hadn't seriously given it thought. His first reaction was no, he couldn't imagine Saralynn agreeing to give up her own space and share his. Not yet anyway. On the other hand, going to bed and waking up together held definite appeal. "I don't think we're there yet. Besides, we'd have to go public first."

"And she doesn't want to."

"We haven't talked about it recently, so I'm not sure, but my gut says no."

"You should talk to her. Make *sure* you're on the same page. Communication is the most important thing in a relationship."

"Okay, Oprah."

"Mock all you want, but which one of us can be seen in public with his girlfriend?"

Well, damn. Kid had a point.

Brownie sundae balanced on one hand, Sandy stopped by the booth across from them and collected the meager tip those diners had left with a soft sigh under her breath. She replaced the disappointment with a smile when she presented Cole with his dessert.

"This looks awesome. Thank you." A second after that, the captain attacked the plate with his spoon.

"You are very welcome. Anything else I can get you?"

"You've been excellent, Sandy, just a check whenever you can. And on behalf of all customers, I'd like to apologize for the crappy tip those people left you." Having waited tables in his teens, Madden knew how tips could make or break a day. Sure, he'd grown up financially stable, but his father had insisted he get a job as soon as he could drive. Something about idle hands. Any spending money had depended on his tips.

"Oh." She flushed under the fluorescents, clearly surprised and embarrassed that he'd noticed. "One low tip doesn't make much difference. Bills just pile up so fast, it's hard to stay on top of things. Most times I don't realize something's due until I get a late notice."

"I know how that can be. You think you're managing well, but things happen. If you don't mind a little advice, something that worked for me was making a list of all my expenses and when everything was due. Look at it every day, and you'll never forget again. Makes budgeting easier, too. Once you have that list, you could also set up monthly text or email alerts."

"Are you an accountant?"

"A couple lifetimes ago." After having been in the paper a number of times—none of which were flattering—it was refreshing to talk to someone who had no idea who he was. "Plus, I've been in debt." Serious, obscene debt. "I know how scary it can be and how good it feels to climb out."

"You should consider opening a debt consulting business. I bet you have a lot of good advice. And in this city, I'm sure you'd have a lot of clients."

He smiled and nodded. The thought of running his own business, and one that helped people, was tempting. But he already had a job he loved. If only he were allowed to do it.

Chapter Seventeen

Saturday, March 15th

All week. All week they'd been trading secret glances and smiles, brushing against each other in the hallway but not talking. They'd both been too busy with an extra-heavy game week, and it was starting to get to her. So when Madden sent her a text on Friday formally asking for a date, she'd typed "Yes!" so hard, she almost cracked her screen. *Easy, girl.* She insisted on hosting this time. Neither her apartment nor her cooking would make the impression he had the week before, but she could make up for that. Hopefully.

She'd never been the eager one in a relationship, and she would have felt off balance if he weren't eager as well. And she knew he was because he'd been texting her all day. When guys had done that in the past, it was annoying, suffocating, a turnoff. Those guys weren't Madden.

What was happening to her? *I miss you* and *I can't wait to see you* used to give her a headache. Now they gave her the warm and fuzzies. The proof was in the hours it took her to get ready, most of that time spent picking an outfit. Her first instinct was to go sexy, but she didn't want to look desperate, so she opted for an outfit that was sultry but didn't scream "needy."

She lit taper candles on the dining table in her cozy kitchen and straightened the place settings. The oven beeped at the same time Madden knocked, and she called over her shoulder, "It's open!" Silly anticipation surged through her, though she tried to tamp it down as she lifted the casserole dish onto the stove.

She waved him in, but he just stood in the doorway, blank shock on his face. "When you said you'd take care of dinner, I thought you meant order a pizza. You cooked? For me?"

"You cooked for *me*." She planted a hand on her waist, but some of the intended sass might've been lost thanks to the oven mitt. At least it was Vera Bradley.

He laughed and held his hands palms out. "No woman's ever cooked for me before. And that smells so good, I'm ready to sell my soul for some."

"Are you serious?" It seemed unlikely no woman had ever made a meal for Madden Vaughn. Unless they were too busy making a meal *of* him. Some of her spunk drained away. "Guess we're even. You're my first in the kitchen."

A fire lit behind his eyes, yet along with it was the gooey, dewy adoration that should've scared her to death but instead warmed the dark parts of her heart. She tried to play it off with a shrug. "It's just mac and cheese, but it's my specialty. Annnnd ... " She tilted a pot sideways so he could see the chili-like mixture inside. "Sloppy joes."

"Marry me." He said it straight-faced even though she knew it was a joke, and yet, the bottom fell out of her stomach, and goose bumps covered her arms. *Stupid, traitorous body.*

"You might want to hold off until you taste it, but I'm pretty confident."

Madden took a seat while she piled the sloppy joe on buns and set one on each of their plates. The mac and cheese she set in the middle of the table then slid into her own chair. "*Bon appetit.*"

His gaze pored over the food for a good three seconds before he even reached for the casserole. He piled some on his plate and breathed deep through his nose, making a pleased animal sound in his throat. "What are the red things?"

"Red bell pepper. Gives it a sweet crunch and lightens up the heavy cheese. Before you ask, the little dots are cayenne pepper for some heat."

At the last two words, he met her eyes and smiled.

Okay, so they didn't need any help with heat, but they had to get through dinner first. She dug in, and the familiar, delicious flavors registered, but she wasn't that hungry for once. Not when all she could think about was what he looked like under the fitted T-shirt. She wanted to know whether Madden wore boxers or briefs more than she wanted her next bite. A year was a long time for a dry spell, but it wasn't just that. They connected on every other level. The sex would have to be electric.

Hard to read his thoughts, but if the way he was devouring the food was any clue, his full focus was on the meal. It was at once a boost and a blow to her ego. All right, she was a good cook, but apparently, she was no competition for mac and cheese and sloppy joes. *God, I'm jealous of food. Get a grip.* She'd been neurotic over a lot of things in her life, but never a man. Is this what all of her dates had felt like?

The clatter of a spoon hitting plate caught her attention. He'd eaten it all. While he went for casserole seconds, she ate as much as she could. By the time he finished again, so had she. Madden wiped his mouth with a napkin then patted his flat stomach. "Best mac I've ever had. I will pay you for that recipe. I'm so full, I'm not sure I even have room for dessert. But I could be persuaded."

Her pulse picked up. Now or never. "I'm glad to hear you say that." She rose and walked around the table to stand in front of him. "Because I had something sweet in mind."

His pupils dilated as he looked up at her, his body tense.

She curled her fingers under the hem of her shirt, sliding it slowly up and over her head before she tossed it aside. His lips parted, but for a nerve-shattering minute, he didn't say anything, just drank her in, paying extra attention to the way she filled out the pink lace bra. What if he still wanted to wait? Self-conscious was a new emotion, and she was not a fan. It took everything to keep from grabbing her top and bolting for the bathroom. "I know you said you wanted to go slow, and if this is too … "

He stood up faster than she could track, and the rest of that sentence didn't matter because his lips were on hers, hot and hungry. He pulled her flush against him, and his hands slid up her back then down her arms as if he couldn't get enough of her, and she understood completely. No matter how close she pressed against him—so close she could feel his heart hammering against hers—it wasn't enough. She slid her hands under his shirt, and the combination of soft warm skin over hard muscle just about took out her legs.

Madden the mind reader curled a hand under each thigh and lifted her legs around his waist. He pulled back from the kiss long enough to pant, "Bedroom?"

"That way." She pointed behind him then took the opportunity to kiss along his jaw and behind his ear while he navigated. When she flicked her tongue *in* his ear, he froze for a second and groaned.

"You keep doing that, and we won't make it to the bed."

Just for fun, she did it again, and he walked a little faster.

• • •

Madden's brain hadn't entirely caught up to what was happening, but that was okay. His body had a pretty good handle on it. One minute he was complimenting her cooking, and the next, somehow she was half-naked in front of him. They'd waited a month and a half. That was slow enough, right? They hadn't just jumped into things. And obviously she was in favor of moving forward.

He tossed her onto the bed, where she landed on the white down comforter with a bounce and a laugh. When she'd wiggled out of her jeans and he was down to his boxers, panic hit. "Oh …"

"Nightstand. I picked some up last night." Her smile was both innocent and wicked, and it turned him on even more.

Once fully protected, he crawled onto the bed and kissed a path from her ankle up the inside of her thigh, over her stomach and between her breasts until he reached her lips. "I think I know, but I have to ask. Are you sure—"

She grabbed his face in both hands and cut him off with a hot kiss, her back arching to press her breasts against his chest. When she broke away, she nipped at his lower lip and whispered, "Yes. I want to know you. Completely."

Dear God, he wanted to know her, too. He reached behind her and unclasped her bra then slid it down her arms and dropped it over the side of the bed. Perfect. She was perfect. He must have stared too long for her liking because she rolled her hips against his and whimpered. He smiled and kissed her again while sliding her panties down to her knees. She helped get them the rest of the way off, and then nothing was between them.

He curled two fingers inside her to see if she was ready, and her warm, slick heat coated them. It didn't look like either of them would last long. He held his weight with a forearm on either side of her and poised himself between her legs. Slow and gentle had been his plan, but she wrapped her legs around his waist and guided him home. They both cried out, and from there, it was a frenzy of kissing, touching, squeezing, and thrusting.

So many heightened sensations hit all at once, it was overwhelming. It felt like floating on a higher plane of existence. He wasn't new to sex, but sex with Saralynn didn't compare to anything in his experience. Maybe it was the sweet, gradual build of anticipation, or never knowing what she'd do at any given moment. Those things definitely added to the rush, but it was more than that.

They were so in sync. Somehow she knew exactly where all of his sensitive spots were and played them to perfection. She kissed behind his ear and at the base of his throat while her hands slid over his hips and down to his thighs. Her fingers dug in, urging him deeper inside her, and he almost lost it. This kind of physical compatibility usually took months to figure out, if ever, but here, now, it was effortless and so much more powerful than ever before.

As she writhed beneath him and her nails found his back, stars exploded behind his eyes. He held onto her hips and moved faster, harder. She held on tighter, her soft, rhythmic moans of encouragement pushing him to the edge, and then he fell over it. He thrust deep one last time. She threw her head back and cried out his name as her body tensed and pulsed around him. He rocked his hips gently while they rode out the blinding sparks before his muscles went slack.

He had just enough presence of mind to hold some of his weight off her until he could roll on his side, pulling her with. While they caught their breaths, he brushed a wild strand of hair behind her ear then traced down her arm to her fingers and lifted them to his lips. "I don't have words for that."

She narrowed her eyes playfully. "Ninety percent of the things you say, I can't tell if they're compliments or digs."

"Sometimes both, but this time, 100 percent compliment."

"Oh. Well, good. We concur then." The relief in her big, dark eyes touched him. When had a woman been concerned about whether or not *he'd* had a good time? Never that he could remember. In fact, he'd always been so focused on ensuring their good time, he hadn't considered until now that his partner might have the same insecurity. If they had, none had ever been brave enough to admit it.

"We concur." He leaned back just enough to admire her body and took his time. They'd been in such a hurry, he'd missed the full tour, and a closer inspection only firmed his opinion. Beautiful. Every inch of her. His gaze stopped on a small tattoo hiding on the inside of her hip. An intricate, filigree heart, green at the top and fading into blue and purple at the bottom. He traced the curling lines with a fingertip.

"It's the only one I have. My family doesn't know and would lose it if they did. They're not fans of body modification of any kind except pierced ears, and even then, it's one hole per ear and only the women. So if you could not mention it to my brother, that'd be great."

He grinned. "Out of everything tonight, you're most worried about Reese finding out about the tattoo."

"He might actually be cool with it, but he'd definitely care how you found out."

"Noted." It seemed like a natural segue into them going public, but he held back. No sense marring the best sex of his life with a heavy conversation that could crack the delicate foundation they were building. Soon, though. This night had only sealed the deal. She was important to him. Their relationship had so much potential it scared him, but the only thing scarier was *not* going for it. If there had ever been a time to go all in, this was it. He'd have to lay everything on the line. But not tonight.

Saralynn studied him the same way he'd taken her in, and her pleased expression said she didn't find him lacking either. "Do you have any tattoos?"

"No. There were some near misses in college, but even drunk, nothing appealed to me enough to have it on my body forever."

"I can appreciate that. I've seen some bad choices. Beer logos, superheroes, cartoons, and never because they had any personal meaning."

"Does yours?"

She touched it almost reflexively, unconsciously. "My grandmother on my mom's side passed when I was five. I don't have a lot of memories of her, just cooking and holidays, and the way she seemed like a kid even at eighty-seven. She had a silver locket my grandpa gave her when they were dating, and she wore it always, even after he died. She left it to me because I loved it. My sisters were jealous, but I wore it every day. I'd wanted a tattoo for a long time, and when I finally turned eighteen, I knew what to get."

He kissed her temple. "I've never seen you wear a locket."

"That's because I gave it to Shiloh under the condition that she had to share it with Sophie. I still have it here. And here." She lifted her hand from the tattoo to her heart.

There was a lot of depth to this woman who cast herself as shallow. He kissed her softly. "I'm sure your grandma would be proud of who you've become."

"I'm trying."

He kissed her again, and she returned it gently at first, but as it lingered, it grew hotter and more insistent. Though he'd been sure the first time had drained him completely, here he was rising to the challenge. After a quick change in protection, he let her take control.

Saralynn laid him back and explored his body with her lips and fingertips at an excruciating pace. When she finally straddled him, he had to ball his fists in the sheets to hold back. The pleasure was intense, and he was enthralled as she planted her palms on his chest and found an exquisite rhythm. He joined in and rocked against her, and when she tossed her head back and gasped, he lost himself all over again.

It was worth every second they'd waited.

Chapter Eighteen

Monday, March 17th

Green was always big around the office since it was one of the Sinners' colors, but on St. Patrick's Day, people went all out. Madden had chosen one of the team's themed holiday shirts with Sinbad the mascot in the middle of a four-leaf clover on the front. He wore it with grass-colored Chuck Taylor sneakers, a hunter green sports jacket, and his usual dark jeans. The rest of the staff looked a little more formal, but that wasn't new. Encouraging, flirty texts from Saralynn had him in a good mood, and he was feeling especially lucky.

He swung into her office and eased the door closed. The bouquet of two dozen white roses sat on her desk. She looked up from her phone call with a grin and held up one finger.

"That's right. A foam finger for the first thousand people in the door tonight and Sinners shamrock shakes at every concession stand. Thanks for checking with me, Pete." She hung up and rounded the desk to kiss him quickly.

He held it for an extra second then nodded to the flowers. "Someone must like you."

"I guess so. No name, but the note said he had a great time with me this weekend. I had a great time with him, too. What is with this getup?" She looked him up and down, but her gaze landed on his green and white striped top hat with clovers around the brim.

"Just getting in the spirit. I'm gonna be on the ground floor at tonight's game, so I wanted to be festive."

"Festive. That's definitely one word for it." Her mouth contorted as she appeared to wrestle with a smile, but she lost. It wasn't even like he could poke fun back at her because she looked hot as ever in a fitted black suit with a silky green shirt that dipped almost too low under the jacket. She took a step forward and hooked a finger into his breast pocket, pulling him down for another kiss. Without a thought, he closed his arms around her waist and soaked in the sweetness of her small frame against his body.

After a minute, she stepped away, and her gaze darted to the door then back to him. She was right. Someone could walk in at any time, but that only made it hotter. He reined it in and tried to turn off all the switches she'd flicked on with his libido. She sat on the edge of her desk, crossed her legs, and nudged his knee with the toe of her green satin pump. "You are goofy and incredibly sweet."

"And you are gorgeous and incredibly perceptive."

She flashed those perfect, white teeth and shook her head.

He slid into one of the chairs facing her desk and, folding his hands across his stomach, thought better of it, and laid his arms on the rests. His heartbeat picked up, and his throat went dry. They had to have this conversation. He couldn't put it off forever. She might even agree.

Saralynn frowned playfully. "What's up with the serious face?"

He took a slow breath. "We've been dating for a while, and our plan was to wait until we knew where it was going before we told anyone. This isn't a passing thing, not for me anyway. I really like you, and I think we have something special. I want to come clean with your brother and my sister. I want to be able to be seen with you in public and not worry about who's going to find out."

Throughout the small speech, Saralynn deflated like a balloon, shrinking in on herself until her head dropped and she stared at her shoes. She didn't say anything for a solid minute, but it felt like ten. It didn't help his nerves. Finally, she lifted her head but focused on a spot across the room. "It's not a passing thing for me either. But we still can't say we know where this is going for sure, and telling them … it could be complicated. We don't know how they'll take it. Can't we just see how things go a little bit longer?"

It hurt to hear even though he'd been expecting it. "We can't hide it from them forever. I don't like keeping secrets from Jacey. I did it for too long, and look where it got me. Now she doesn't believe me even when I'm telling the truth. I want to change that. I have to. And I'm *happy*. I want to be able to share that with the important people in our lives."

She met his gaze, but the pity in hers didn't make him feel better. "I'm sorry. I'm happy, too, but that's why I want to wait. If we tell them, things could get bad. *Really* bad. I'm not exactly Jacey's favorite person after I went behind her back with that press release. I can't imagine she wants us dating, and I'd like her in my corner. This is the first time in my life where I feel like I've found people who appreciate me for who I am. I don't want to lose that."

Part of him understood. After everything she'd been through up to this point, that kind of acceptance would mean a lot. He'd just hoped he meant as much. "I know my sister. She wouldn't lay down that kind of ultimatum. Circumstances were different when Allie and Reese were dating. They were doctor and patient. We're just co-workers."

"I know. But—"

"If you know, then what's holding you back? You don't think what we have rates high enough to tell our families?"

She opened her mouth, but nothing came out. The rock in his gut grew heavier with every silent second. She set a hand on his knee tentatively, like she wasn't sure he wanted it there. If this wasn't a breakup, it felt a hell of a lot like one. "Madden, this past month has been amazing, and I want to keep seeing you. I'm just not ready to go public yet."

"When do you think you will be?"

"After we walk down the aisle? That's not an invitation to propose." She pointed at him, and some lightness had crept into her expression and tone, but it didn't change his mood. She frowned. "I'm sorry. I don't know. I just want to wait until I'm sure that … "

The relationship was worth it? He was worth it? When she still didn't finish the sentence after a minute, he stood. "Let me know when you figure it out."

"Madden … " She followed him to the door, but he kept walking and didn't look back. If he did, he'd cave and give in to whatever she wanted, and he wouldn't fall into old patterns. No more ignoring the signs when a woman wasn't as invested as he was. Why did doing the right thing have to be so damn hard?

• • •

What are you waiting for? Madden had left twenty minutes ago, and she was still asking herself the same stupid question. He'd looked so disappointed. Just when she thought her days of breaking hearts were behind her. Only this time, it broke her heart, too. God, this hurt. Maybe she'd had the right idea, living life on the surface and never letting anyone get close. If a relationship wasn't real, neither was the pain of losing it.

If she was going to give up the best guy she'd ever had for her job, then she might as well do that job. She wiped the corners of her eyes then took a deep breath and opened her inbox. *Shit.* The bachelor auction was this weekend. She'd booked everything months ago then filed it in the back of her mind to make room for the team's day-to-day promotions. Only a few things were left to finalize, but that wasn't the problem. Madden would be there looking *GQ* perfect. And now that she'd turned down going public, what if he brought a date?

The door to her office swung open, and her brother stepped in. Oh yay. This day just kept getting better.

Reese raised his brows at the flowers on her desk. "Whoa, nice. These from radio guy?"

"Yes." Guilt poked her in the chest, but she wasn't about to come clean now.

"You must be pretty serious about this guy. I can't remember the last time you dated someone for more than a month. Have you *ever* dated someone that long?"

"Reese. Did you come in here just to give me a hard time? Because I love you, and you deserve to know that my shit tolerance is pretty low today."

His protective look came out in full effect, creased forehead and concerned eyes with the corners of his mouth dipping down. "What's wrong? Do I need to hurt somebody?"

She squeezed out a shaky smile. "No. But I'm glad that offer's always on the table. It's ... the bachelor auction. Snuck up on me, and I have some last-minute things to get done."

"You'll get 'em done. You always do. Will I finally get to meet radio guy?"

"Oh no, he can't make it."

"Sare. The man sent you two dozen white roses. For St. Patrick's Day. Strikes me as the kind of guy who would make the time. I know you're worried about him meeting me, but I promise I'll be cool. I promise I'll *try* to be cool. Allie will be there. She'll keep me from doing anything over the top."

"I swear. He honestly just—"

"This one seems different. I think you really like him, and if you do, I want to meet him. No hidden motives, no intentions speeches. You're important to me, and I want to get to know who's important to you. My wife informs me I've been replaced as your favorite sibling—not that I can blame you—but you're still *my* favorite."

Ouch. If she believed in signs, this one would meet big, flashy, neon Vegas standards, and it would say *Tell Him Now!* But something held her back. If she told him, she'd have to tell Jacey, and she still wasn't ready to do that. She knew her brother, though. Relationship meddling was a Reese family Olympic sport. It wasn't like she'd stayed out of his and Allie's business when they needed the push to go on their first date. He wasn't going to let this go.

"Okay. I'll bring him."

He unleashed the dopey, big brother smile that made him her true and forever favorite and strode over to hug her with rib-crushing intensity from behind her chair.

"Okay, okay," she wheezed and tapped his arm. "Lungs deflating."

He eased up and kissed the top of her head. "Love you."

"And I love you. Knuckle-dragger."

He winked and left, closing the door behind him. As soon as she was alone, she folded her arms on top of her desk and dropped her face into them. Keeping things under wraps was the best thing for now, wasn't it? Assuming there still *was* something to keep under wraps and Madden wouldn't break up with her. Had they broken up? One thing was for sure. He wouldn't be happy seeing her with some random guy at the auction.

At least she'd never had trouble finding random guys.

Chapter Nineteen

Okay, so maybe finding her date at a local improv class wasn't the best idea, but it seemed better than picking someone up in a bar. At least in an improv class, you found people who wanted to masquerade as someone else. And all it had cost her was ten dollars, a half hour of her life, and some dignity. All right, a lot of dignity.

The tables were set, centerpieces artfully arranged, the sound system checked. When she finished marking off everything on her list, she stowed it behind the DJ's table and took a minute to convince herself the whole night wouldn't blow up in her face. That was a tall order, so she settled for hoping her fake date could stay in character for the next two hours. Speaking of, he'd be in the hotel lobby any minute.

Time to face her fate.

The lobby was already full of early guests mingling and eyeing the ballroom doors. It would have been hard to find her escort if he weren't wearing a cobalt blue satin suit. With matching hair. *Why me?* She kept a public-pretty smile in place as she approached him, took his elbow, and kissed his cheek so she could talk in his ear. "You didn't look like this on Thursday."

"I made a character choice. It totally fits the vibe of a radio station dude, don't you think? Edgy."

"Blake. You look like the Cookie Monster. Look, it's fine. It's just one night of mingling and dancing. You remember the details I gave you?"

"Your brother is Shane Reese. Way cool by the way. I'm a big fan. Maybe if this night goes well, we can—"

"Blake."

"Right, sorry. I work as an assistant at Mix 94.1 and met you when you had players at the station for interviews. We've been dating for a little more than a month, and I sent you two dozen white roses."

"Good. Now just smile and let me do most of the talking."

"A woman who takes charge. I like it."

Just make it through the night. Just make it through the night. "Let's find my brother so we can get that over with. Hold on." She crossed back to the ballroom doors to open and secure them before lifting her voice over the din. "Thank you, everyone, for coming. You're welcome to go in and find your table then pick up a cocktail at the bar."

The glitzy crowd flowed past her, and, for a second, she hoped Blake would get sucked into it and disappear, but no. He hung back and offered her his arm when everyone had gone inside. She accepted and scanned the room for Reese. He and Allie weren't in the initial influx.

"Why don't we get a drink?"

Alcohol. Yes. "Good idea." She steered them toward the bar, and ten minutes and two cosmopolitans later, her nerves were coated.

"Hey, Sare. This must be your guy."

Holy mother of mercy. Apparently her nerves weren't as coated as she thought. Reese's voice over her shoulder almost made her drop her glass. She recovered before she faced him with the best smile in her depleted arsenal. "Yes, Blake, this is my brother Shane—boy, does that sound wrong. Just call him Reese. That vision behind him is my sister-in-law, Allie. Guys, this is my … this is Blake. From the radio station."

"Glad to meetcha. I'm actually just working at the station until I can break onto the Strip. My real passion is magic." Blake shook their hands with enthusiasm. For a split second, Saralynn felt her eyes bulge like they might pop out of her skull. That was *not* in the script. Her own fault. Find a guy at improv, expect him to improvise. If Reese was surprised, he hid it well. Allie, not so much, which was saying a lot for a psychologist. She stared, her mouth hanging open slightly with pure bewilderment.

"Well, hey. We're all at the same table, so why don't we find our seats and get acquainted before the shindig starts?" Reese lifted his brows amiably. To his credit, he was taking all this shockingly well. He must have really meant what he said in her office. Still, how cool would he be if Blake happened to be Madden? Odds were, that scenario would play out entirely differently.

"You know what? I need to make a quick stop by the ladies' room. Sare, why don't you come with me?" Allie tilted her head toward the restrooms with a pointed look.

And leave Reese and Blake alone? That did *not* sound like a good idea. "Oh, I'm okay. I think I'll head over with the guys—"

"Please? Do a girl a favor. I'm afraid there won't be a place to hang my wrap and purse, and I don't want to put them on the floor. I'd leave them with Shane, but I want to freshen up while I'm in there. Powder my nose." She was playing dirty. Saralynn couldn't say no now, and they both knew it.

"Okay. Sure. We'll just be a minute." She smiled at her brother then met Blake's gaze and tried to send a telepathic threat. *Do not say anything stupid. Stick to the plan.* Blake winked and waved. Why wasn't that reassuring?

Allie took her elbow, and when they were far enough away, yelled as quietly as a person could yell, "Are you out of your mind? What are you doing? Who is that?"

"That's Blake."

"Want to try again?"

"Okay." Saralynn sighed and glanced back. The two men were talking at the table. Blake with expressive arms. Jesus. "Madden sent me flowers on Monday. Reese came in and saw them. As far as he knows, I've been dating a guy from the radio station. A nonexistent guy. He kept on about how he wanted to meet this man, and I knew he wouldn't get off my back unless I let him."

"So you ... "

"Went fishing in an improv class. Hooked Blake. For the record, he did *not* look like that when I met him."

"Oh okay. Because that makes it all copasetic. What does Madden think about this?"

"That's the other thing. Before Reese came in, Madden said he wanted to tell everybody about us. I said I wasn't ready. He asked when I would be, and I didn't have an answer. He left pretty upset."

"I'll bet he did. Have you talked to him since then?"

Saralynn pinched her lips together and shook her head.

"So he doesn't know about Papa Smurf over there." Allie's face contorted as she tried not to laugh but ended up snorting. "I'm sorry. It's really not funny. This could end very, very badly."

"Your job is to make people feel better about themselves, right?"

"Not really. I shed light on situations. Get people to see what they can't or won't on their own so they can do the right thing and improve their lives. Happy ending, painful process."

"Awesome."

Allie nudged her out of the flow of traffic and found them a shadowed spot against the wall. "Your process is turning out more painful than most because you keep creating hurdles. Like Little Boy Blue."

"He was *normal-colored* when I met him."

"Again. Not the point. This is Vegas. These people have seen weirder. If Shane can accept a freak like Blaze—"

"Blake."

"Blake. If Shane can accept *him*, why do you think he'd lose it over Madden?"

Saralynn glanced back to their table, where her brother appeared a thoughtful listener as Blake told a story and mimed pulling a rabbit out of a hat. Dear God. It *would* have been different with Madden, right? He'd been included in the talk Reese had given to every man in Las Vegas Arena about staying away from her.

"Madden was a groomsman because Shane *likes* him. You're not giving your brother enough credit. He's watched you evolve, and he's changed. He's proud of you."

"But Jacey—"

"Isn't going to fire you. Not for that. You've single-handedly raised team awareness by at least fifty percent in the year you've been here. The Sinners mobile app you developed will buy you at least one more season as long as you don't do something like pose for *Playboy* or hit someone with your car. There's one very obvious reason for the hurdles. I'll let you think about that. I really do have to use the restroom, and it looks like you need to start the show."

Players were filing backstage, ready to be auctioned. Even Reese had excused himself from Blake, who was now talking to … *oh no.* What was Madden doing at their table? His expression went from amiable and curious to dark and brooding the more Blake talked. He nodded, said something, then disappeared into the crowd. She took two steps before someone caught her wrist, and then Allie's voice was in her ear.

"Later. They're waiting on you."

The pull was so strong it felt like she might split right down the middle so each half could go in a separate direction. But Allie was right. Against every one of her instincts, Madden would have to wait. *I did this. I'm the hurdle-maker.* Now was so not the time for self-revelation—or flagellation for that matter—there'd be plenty of opportunity for that later. She closed her eyes and cleared her mind before grabbing a microphone and jogging up on stage.

"Ladies and gentlemen, I'm the master of ceremonies, Saralynn Reese, and I'd like to welcome you to the third annual Sinners' bachelor auction! I hope you're enjoying your drinks and the hors d'oeuvres floating around. Once we divvy up these gorgeous men, we can get to dinner!"

The female portion of the audience broke into cheers, applause, and even whistles as they picked up their paddles.

"All right, ladies, I'd like to remind you we've got some married men up here, so this isn't necessarily to make a love connection. They've generously donated their time, company, and conversation for the evening in return for your generous donation to the Sinners' favorite charity, the children's hospital."

Applause from the whole room now, but not as wild.

"However, if you happen to get one of our true bachelors and hit it off, what you do after dinner is officially none of my business." She threw in a wink, and the whistles and cheers returned with a few catcalls. She scanned the crowd, trying to find Madden, but no luck. "Let's get started then. First up … " She glanced offstage to the bachelor waiting in the wings. "I don't think this guy needs any introduction. It's our captain, Dylan Cole!"

Cole walked out to a deafening reception. One hundred women between the ages of eighteen and sixty lost their minds like tweenagers at a boy band concert. He smiled but kept glancing away from the audience, and sweat beaded on his forehead. The stage lights were hot, but that wasn't it.

Saralynn lifted a hand to quiet the room. "Okay. I know you're excited, but let's not scare the poor guy. He's from a small town in Nova Scotia, so let's be gentle with him."

Some tension drained from his body, and he smiled his gratitude at her then turned that charm on the crowd. He lunged into some weightlifting poses, stretching his tux to its limits. He was barely containing his laughter, but it sent every woman in the room into frenzy. So much for controlling the crowd.

"All right. Okay. That's enough, Arnold." She tugged on his sleeve until he stood straight beside her and the roar in the room died down. Where was Madden? Did he leave? "I'm going to start the bidding at $1,000 because I feel like that's a safe—" Every paddle in the crowd went up. "That's what I thought. Show me $1,500." Most stayed. "How about $2,000?" A third of the remaining dropped out. "What about $2,500?" Only a handful of paddles left. "Anyone for $3,000? Remember, this isn't just for the player but the children's hospital." Two paddles stayed in the air. "Thank you, ladies. Well, $3,500?"

One paddle lowered. The winner jumped out of her seat and did a touchdown dance, spiking an imaginary football with butterfly knees all in a very expensive-looking evening gown and high heels. The crowd applauded and laughed, and Cole bowed his thanks for the woman's donation.

As he strode off the stage to his excited date, Saralynn searched the sea of people again for Madden. *Please tell me he didn't leave. Please.* And then she saw him. Arms folded across his chest in the back of the room by the bar. Hard to tell for sure from this distance, but he looked pissed. That was okay. Pissed she could deal with. As long as he didn't leave.

• • •

Where the hell had she found *Blake*? The guy was so not her type. Or anyone's type on Earth. If she was trying to send Madden a message, it was damn well received. A whole week without hearing from her had been hard, but he'd given her space. Time to think. But apparently she'd never been serious about him at all if she'd been seeing Blake the whole time. Over a month he'd said.

Well, that was it. He was done. No more dating for the foreseeable future. He loosened his bow tie and unbuttoned his suit jacket. If he left early, Jacey would assume he met someone, and the future Mrs. Blake the Great wouldn't notice at all. He reached in his pocket for car keys then stopped. Saralynn wrapped up the auction, and as she walked down the stage steps, the long skirt of her dress parted in the middle to reveal long, slender legs that he had carnal memories of.

He couldn't help staring as she wound through the crowd to her table, looking like Miss America minus the crown, and he wasn't the only one who noticed. Heads turned in her wake, but she seemed oblivious. The DJ called all bachelors and their dates to the dance floor as well as anyone else who might be interested. Blake stood and held out his hand. Saralynn hesitated, looked around, then took it and followed him to the middle of the room.

I should just go. But then Blake set his hands low on Saralynn's back—too low—and impulse got the better of Madden. He scanned the place, not sure what he was looking for until he saw Allie sitting alone at her table. She was the one person Saralynn talked to. Reese was out for his obligatory dance with his date for the night. It was worth a shot. Before the idea even fully formulated, he was headed straight for the new Mrs. Reese. When he stopped beside her, Allie looked up, and her eyes widened.

He held out his arm. "Dance?"

She glanced at Saralynn and Blake, and her face suggested a million thoughts were running through her brain, but he couldn't guess any of them. Finally, she nodded and curled her hand around his elbow. He took the first spot he could find on the periphery of the dance floor and pulled Allie to him but kept his hands in as respectful and platonic places as he could find.

She remained stiff but followed his lead and avoided his eyes for the first minute. He managed to catch her gaze, and the pity there had him ready to leave again. But her hands tightened on his shoulders, and she mouthed "not real," tilting her head toward Saralynn and Blake.

He leaned down so she could talk in his ear. "It's a show for Shane. He wanted to meet her boyfriend, so she found an actor. Talk to her. This isn't about you."

"How do you know?"

She gave him a look that said, *How do you think?*

Oh, right. Psychologist. Word was, you could spend five minutes with Allie and she'd be able to tell you why you always ate Lucky Charms for breakfast instead of eggs and toast, voodoo like that. "Okay, but—"

Blake's hands slid south and squeezed. Saralynn tried to push him away, but he held on and moved in for a kiss. She wrenched her head to the side and tried to wrestle out of his grip but was losing. Madden didn't think. He let Allie go, took three strides, and punched Blake across the jaw. Not hard enough to break anything, but hard enough to make him stumble back, stunned.

"Are you okay?" he asked Saralynn.

She stared at him, hands over her mouth, in horror, surprise, and if he wasn't mistaken, a bit of admiration. She glanced around at the people watching them, lowered her arms, and regained her cool. "Yeah. Thanks. It's okay. We're fine." Those last two comments were for the gawkers, who gradually resumed dancing. Blake stomped past mumbling, "Fuck this, man. Not worth it."

Reese appeared next, looking primed for violence himself. "What happened? What'd he do?"

"Nothing. It's fine." Saralynn set a hand on her brother's arm, but it didn't appear to do the job.

"He took some liberties he shouldn't have," Madden said. My reaction was a little strong. I don't like to see guys take advantage."

Reese nodded his approval then studied his sister and frowned like he was trying to work something out. Allie stepped in and took her husband's arm. "Let's just be glad everyone's okay. You have a date to get back to, and a second cocktail is calling my name." She smiled and kissed him, and after a second, he kissed her nose. The woman was good. Sometimes scary good. Did they all do that distraction thing?

Madden didn't have time to think too much about it because a small hand clamped on his wrist and tugged. He followed Saralynn to the back of the room, where she pulled him into a shadow against the wall. Before he could get a word out, she pointed at him. "Ask me if I brought you here to make out and I'll punch *you*."

He blinked and held his hands up in defense. "Okay. Why *did* you bring me here?"

"What was that back there? I didn't need you to step in and save me. I had it handled."

"You're kidding, right? Maybe I shouldn't have done what I did, but that guy way overstepped. And while we're on it, who the hell was he? Allie said you hired an actor. For Reese?"

That took away some of her steam.

"The truth, Saralynn. You owe me that much."

"Reese came in right after you did on Monday. He wouldn't let up about meeting the only man I've ever dated for more than a month."

"So instead of using that as an opportunity to be honest … "

"I created a slimy Smurf hurdle." She must have read his confusion because she waved away her previous statement and rushed on. "I know I should have handled it better, but I panicked. I found Blake to play my boyfriend for one night."

"So you'd rather pretend to date that thing than admit to seeing me."

"No … I … you had to have been in my head at the time. I warned you when we started. I'm bad at this. Catastrophically bad. I'm learning, but given my past, there's a hell of a curve. I don't want to date or pretend to date anyone but you. I just need you to be patient."

I've been an asshole. He did know, going in, that this was new ground for them both. Things had gone so well, it had been so effortless, he'd forgotten. "I can do that. I'm sorry. I didn't mean to pressure you. But considering tonight, I still think—"

"I know. I want to tell them. Can I do it, though? Reese will definitely take it better from me, and I think Jacey would respect me more if I came forward instead of hiding behind you."

The weight he'd carried for the last week disappeared. He pulled her close and kissed her for all he was worth. She squeaked, then he felt her smile before she kissed him back. One of her bare legs parted the slit in her dress and found its way between his legs, and he moaned. Everything in the background faded away until a deep, familiar voice broke through.

"Got over Blake pretty fast.

Saralynn jumped a foot away, her face painted with guilt and panic. Madden braced himself, squared his shoulders, and turned to Reese. He had nothing to apologize for.

"What the hell, Sare? I thought you were supposed to be past this kind of crap, but at least now things are making sense. I had my doubts about the aspiring magician, but you dated stranger in your teens, so I let it go. Except then the guy you'd supposedly been dating for a month and were crazy about makes a douche bag move, and Madman here sweeps in like your great protector. I'll talk to *you* later, by the way."

"No you won't." Saralynn faced off with her brother, chin angled up, but she kept her voice low. "I'm not a baby anymore. I can make my own decisions, and you don't get to decide who I date. Yes, I've been seeing Madden. And this is exactly why I didn't want to tell you."

"Sare ... " Reese sighed. "Did it occur to you I might be upset *because* you didn't tell me? We've always been close. Closer since you moved here. Is it too much to want to be kept in the loop?"

"If your inclusion comes with judgment and lectures, then yes."

Before Reese could respond, Allie tapped his shoulder. "Your date's looking for you. And I don't mean me. Sorry to interrupt, but this might be better to discuss at another time anyway."

Reese dipped out of her touch and headed for their table. Allie slid a hand over her face. "It's only a matter of time until he realizes I knew about this all along, so tomorrow should be fun."

"Allie, I'm sorry."

"You want to make it up to me? Make it up to him." She tilted her head in Reese's direction then followed after him.

Saralynn closed her eyes.

Madden caught her hand and squeezed it. "We'll fix this. It'll be okay." Except they still had to tell his sister before it became common knowledge, and she'd been stressed lately, not quite her normal, understanding self. He wouldn't say it out loud, but maybe Saralynn had been right.

Chapter Twenty

This close to the playoffs, there was only one place to catch Shane Reese for sure. It also happened to be the worst possible venue for the discussion they needed to have, but Madden didn't have a choice. Reese was best friends with Carter, and from there, it was a short step to Jacey. Since Saralynn wanted the honor of telling his sister about their relationship, he couldn't duck out of this conversation.

I should have worn a cup.

He hung to the side of the locker room, in shadow, and went unnoticed as practice let out. Guys filed past him, lost in conversation, cell phones, or headphones. Good. Nealy, the head coach, walked out, staring at her clipboard, and he held his breath. She made it halfway down the hall and paused. *Jesus, please keep going.* She was a tiny woman, but she put the fear of God in everyone she met. Professionally, anyway. Most likely, she wouldn't care about two executives dating each other, but she was close with Jacey, like a guard dog who smelled fear and delighted in it. She turned a fraction, made a dismissive noise, and left through the underground garage. Madden nearly slid down the wall.

No one left except … the locker room door swung open, and Reese hustled out, car keys jingling in his hand.

"Hey."

Reese's shoulders bunched before he turned around. "Hey, Vaughn. Stop by to give me a heart attack? Another one?"

"I wanted to say I'm sorry."

"You're sorry. That could cover a whole lot of ground. What are you sorry for? Disregarding my request and dating my sister?" His request. That was almost funny. It had been a damn order. Reese's rigid posture said a physical confrontation was still a possibility, so Madden hung back.

"No."

Reese cocked his head to the side.

"I'm not sorry for dating Saralynn."

"I love my sister, but you're the first ex-boyfriend who's ever said that."

"Not ex. Cut her a break. She's not the same person."

"No? She dated a guy in secret, lied about it, and went to extreme measures to cover it up. Sounds like the same Sare to me." He glanced at the locker room. "Sure you want to talk about this here? You know, Cole's still in there."

"Yeah … " It took everything in him to hold back a wince. "It's okay. He knows."

"*He* knows."

"That's what I'm sorry for. We're friends, and I should have been upfront with you. Dude, I like you and I respect you. I was in your wedding. I didn't want to go behind your back. But considering the speech you gave everyone when Saralynn started, I knew your stance on it. I had every intention of keeping my word, but then … "

Something changed in Reese's expression. He looked almost sympathetic. "Yeah. I've seen that look. Followed not too long after by utter devastation. I know how she can be. I didn't warn you guys away from her for *her* benefit." He placed a flat hand over his heart. "Again. Baby sister, and she means the world to me. She can do anything. Except relationships."

"Can't say I've had the best luck myself. But I'm trying this time. So is she."

Reese went quiet for a minute like he was thinking it over. Or sizing him up for a coffin, hard to tell. Finally, he nodded. "You've made it longer than any of the others; I'll say that. So you came here why? For my blessing?"

"Not exactly. I mean, I want you to be cool with this. That would mean a lot. But I'm gonna keep seeing her either way."

"Ballsy. I'm torn between respecting that and wanting to kick your ass."

"I get it. Believe me. I'm here because Jacey doesn't know yet, and Saralynn wants to tell her."

Reese looked at him like he'd sprouted another head. "Okay. First, you have bigger problems than me if Jacey doesn't know. She's been a little unpredictable lately. I'm glad I wasn't the only one in the dark on this, but shit, man. Good luck. Second, and I can't believe I heard this right, Saralynn wants to tell her?"

"She thinks Jace'll respect her more. I offered, but she said she doesn't want to hide behind me."

"Saralynn said that? Saralynn Reese? 'Bout yea high, big, Bambi eyes, with a way of making you agree to something before you realize you're doing it?"

Madden grinned. "That's her."

"That's … " He shook his head. "That's amazing. You're right. She has changed. Allie kept telling me, and I should have listened. There's no better judge of personality than my wife, but I thought Sare had bewitched her like everyone else. I'm the idiot here. My sister still went overboard with the cover-up, but I understand a little better now."

"So you won't—"

"No. I won't say anything. Not to Jacey. But I need to apologize to my sister."

"Thanks, man."

Reese hesitated then held out his hand. "I'm glad we talked."

"Me too."

"If we *have* fallen into this parallel universe you describe where Saralynn doesn't break up with you first, you should know I'll break you in half if you hurt her."

It wasn't an idle threat. He could do it. And hell, Madden had made the same threat to Carter two years ago when he and Jace were still pretending not to love each other. It was a brother thing. "Understood."

The goalie nodded and disappeared down the hall. Madden released a breath he hadn't realized he'd been holding. That went surprisingly well. If Reese could be okay with it, maybe Jacey would too. Sure. And maybe Vegas would lose the casinos in favor of a family fun park, and trade showgirls for cuddly, G-rated character mascots. Suddenly he was grateful Saralynn wanted to dive in front of this particular bullet.

Chapter Twenty-One

When delivering bad news, it always helped to cushion it with good news. The tricky part was making sure the good news trumped the bad. At least, that's how Saralynn planned on coming clean with Jacey and keeping her job. She stood from behind her desk and pulled out her earbuds, sufficiently pumped on high-octane pop music, and knocked on Jacey's door, still humming "One Girl Revolution."

"It's open."

She walked in, head high and heart beating like a jackhammer. "Hi. Do you have a minute?"

"Sure. Have a seat." Jacey finished signing a document. "What can I do for you?"

Saralynn closed the door then eased into the chair opposite Jacey's desk, her posture straight from years of dance training. She tried to keep her hands loose in her lap. Not that she had a ton of experience, but it felt like sitting in the principal's office. Guilt weighed on her even though she hadn't really done anything wrong. "Well, I just wanted to tell you I've been—"

"Dating my brother."

Even for someone practiced in maintaining a cool expression, that one threw her, and her mouth fell open but only for a second.

Jacey smiled, but it wasn't exactly happy. "I didn't know for sure, but the pieces fit. It's fine. It's not an ethics breech, and Madden can date whomever he wants. Just keep it professional at work."

"I ... of course." It couldn't be that easy, could it? She'd had a whole speech planned out with bullet points and everything. Jacey wasn't doing a jig or welcoming her to the family, but she wasn't writing up a pink slip either. This reaction was better than she could have hoped for. So why did it feel disappointing?

Maybe because it wasn't approval but more like acceptance. *Madden can date whomever he wants.* The lack of concern, or at least curiosity, felt off. It underlined the rift between Jacey and Madden, and that tightness in her chest? Another sympathy pang for the man who was starting to mean more to her than she knew how to handle.

"Is that all?"

Saralynn jolted back into the moment. "No, actually. I've been getting a lot of letters—a *lot* of letters—from female fans about the dance team. They think it's demeaning and ridiculous, and out of place at a hockey game."

Jacey closed her eyes and rubbed her forehead. "I know. I don't disagree, but I was out-voted two years ago, and they did give us a boost in ticket sales. Besides that, they provide other important functions like T-shirt and concession giveaways. They host team meet-and-greets and do birthday parties for fans."

"Right. They need to stay. But I was thinking, to add some validity, we could have them do shootouts and play three-on-three mini games during period breaks. They could even wear our new women's jerseys and potentially increase those sales. We could work it like any other mid-game promotion and pick two seating sections. Say, if one team of ladies wins, section 103, row M gets free pizza, if the other team wins, another row gets it."

"That's a really good idea. It could show that the dance team has some skill and hockey knowledge and isn't just there for decoration. Nice work. I like it. There are some logistics issues though. They had to know how to skate to make the dance team, but how many of those girls know how to shoot a puck? I don't want them out there scrambling around, looking like a joke. That could make things worse."

"Totally agree. That's why I want to run some clinics. I was going to ask Coach Windham if she'd mind sparing an hour after each team practice for a week."

Jacey tilted her chin up like she was going to say something, but at the mention of the Sinners' coach, she pressed her lips together and looked like she was holding back a laugh. Understandable. Nealy Windham had a reputation for scaring the shit out of her players—tough, enormous men. God knows what she'd do to a dance team. But if they needed to learn hockey, there was no better teacher than Nealy. Jacey cleared her throat. "Okay. Um. Good luck."

Saralynn saluted and stood. "So you're on-board with this?"

"On-board. Oh, Saralynn?"

She paused on her way out the door and looked over her shoulder.

"Be careful. With Madden. Workplace romances can be complicated, and you're a real asset to this team. I wouldn't want anything to jeopardize that."

Her proud buzz took a nosedive as she tried to separate the compliment from the insinuation that her relationship would probably fail. At a loss, she just nodded and saw herself out. *Be careful with Madden.* Because *she* was the one likely to screw things up? Maybe that's not what Jacey meant. Not that it wasn't a legitimate concern. After all, she'd almost crashed and burned their love boat on an iceberg named Blake just this past weekend. But things were out in the open now, and it would be different. No more hiding or hurdles, and damned if she wouldn't prove that to Madden, to Jacey, and most of all, to herself.

She ducked into her office and ran right into her brother's back. "Reese." She rubbed her nose. "Now's not a good time."

He turned around and smirked but just as fast traded it for an apologetic expression. "I'm sorry, Sare."

"No biggie. I should have watched where I was going."

"No, I mean for Saturday night. For everything. Madden came and talked to me yesterday after practice. I like to think I'm pretty intimidating, but he didn't back down. I respect that. He's a good guy, and I'm sorry I made you feel like you couldn't tell me."

She tried to imagine Madden going toe to toe with her big brother and smiled. Facing off with Reese was no small feat. No guy had ever done that for her before. It should have felt good. And it did on some deep, basic level. So why did she have the sudden urge to run away for a week by herself on some remote island? No doubt Allie would have the answers, but Saralynn didn't, so she hugged her brother to avoid talking it out. Reese might be all evolved and ready to listen, but she wasn't ready for more self-excavation at the moment. He tucked his chin on top of her head like he'd always done. With everything that had been going on, she hadn't even realized how much she'd missed him.

"You all right?"

"Yeah. I'm fine."

"Never in recorded history has fine ever meant fine coming from a woman."

"Stop worrying about me. I can take care of myself." Said the girl clinging to a hug from her big brother. She stepped back.

"Sorry. Worrying's in the job description. Sure you're okay?"

"I'm cool. I'm great. I'm awesome. And I'm way behind on a project for Friday. Catch you later?"

He studied her like he wasn't convinced, but he was smart enough to back off. "Yeah, okay. Love you."

"Love you back."

When he left, she fell into her chair and stared at the filing cabinet. By all accounts, she should be happy. She was doing well at work, seemingly well in her relationship. Things were out in the open with no dramatic kickback. So where was this anxiety coming from?

What's wrong with me?

Chapter Twenty-Two

For once, Madden actually hoped Cole would be around as he pulled up the horseshoe drive to the enormous mansion, but the house was dark. He didn't feel like being alone, and he needed to think out loud with the possibility of getting an answer back. He'd expected Jacey to have *some* kind of reaction, but according to Saralynn, it was apathy with the caveat that they keep it out of the office.

His sister kept building the wall higher and higher between them, and he had to get through. Jacey was the only family he had left. Losing her wasn't an option. He pulled into the garage and frowned. No lights on, but Cole's SUV was in its spot. Maybe he was watching a movie. Madden headed past the laundry room for the kitchen and threw his keys on the counter. "Honey, I'm home."

Silence. Okay, this was creepy. "Yo! Cole!" Nothing. Oops. What if he'd brought Tricia over? Maybe the two of them were in Cole's room, hoping he'd go away. They usually worked out that kind of thing ahead of time, but it was possible. Only one way to be sure. He went up the marble stairs in the foyer, holding his breath. One good thing about stone—it didn't creak. Blue TV light shone underneath Cole's door, and muted sounds came from inside, but not the carnal kind. There was music, but filtered like it was coming from headphones, and the occasional ... whimper?

Oh man. He was so not suited for this. He turned to leave the guy alone but stopped. Is that what best friends did? How many times had Cole listened to his sob stories? He at least had to offer. Shit. Madden winced and knocked a few times. The music cut out.

"Cole? You okay, man?"

More sounds from inside. Cole blowing his nose, the bed creaking, and then the door opened. His eyes were red and puffy, but he made an effort to look casual. He must have realized how badly he failed because he laughed and slid a hand over his face. "Well, this is fucking embarrassing."

"Remember who you're talking to. The embarrassment bar is pretty high. Nobody else needs to know. What happened?"

He ducked his head, clearly trying not to cry again. "Tricia broke things off."

Damn. What was the protocol here? Dudes didn't hug unless they were saying hello or goodbye, and even then with a handclasp between them. Absolutely not when any emotion was involved. "Do you want to grab a beer from the fridge, kill some zombies? Talk or not talk?"

Cole looked back inside his dark room then nodded. "Yeah. Yeah, that sounds good."

They made a trek through the kitchen to pick up a six-pack then headed for the theater room. It was a little awkward, but Cole seemed steadier, and that felt good. Madden had never had a little brother and never wanted one, but since Cole moved in, he'd seen what he'd missed. It was rewarding to look out for him, to pay him back for all his advice and support.

They sat in their usual spots and each cracked a beer. Madden powered up the projector and game system and waited for it to load or Cole to say something—whichever came first.

"I didn't see it coming at all."

Madden nodded. It was best to let the kid unload in his own time. Besides, what could he say? Only hearing Cole's side of it, it'd sounded like the two had a perfect relationship. Of course he was blindsided.

"Things seemed so great, you know? I guess looking back, she wasn't that excited when I brought up moving in. And maybe she didn't text me as much this past week. I honestly didn't notice with all the games we've been playing and the bachelor auction. That sounds bad, doesn't it?"

"No. You're one of the busiest people I know. And you've been dating her for a few months; she knew your schedule going into it. What'd she say?"

"She met someone else. I asked who, but she said it wasn't important. She said he had more time for her. How could I argue with that? My life is what it is. I did the best I could."

That much was beyond question. Dylan Cole did his best in every area of his life. He wasn't capable of anything less. If Tricia couldn't see or respect that, he deserved better. "I'm sorry, man. This is really rough. I know you cared about her a lot and it doesn't seem like it now, but if that's how she feels, she's not right for you. I happen to know there are millions of other girls who would sell a kidney to be with you. Your fan clubs are proof of that."

Cole laughed. "Yeah, I don't think so. They kinda scare me."

"Okay, they're a little extreme, but you get the point. I promise you there's someone out there."

"Thanks." He took a long pull of beer and stared straight ahead for a minute before refocusing. "What about you? How'd Jacey take the news?"

"She already knew. That shouldn't surprise me. Observation has always been one of her things. Other than that, Saralynn said she didn't seem to care at all. I've been trying to get a minute with Jace all week, but she keeps blowing me off. She's been mad at me before, but she's never frozen me out like this. I just wish I knew what I did that was so bad."

"She knows you didn't gamble, so it can't be that, right? Do you think she's more upset about Saralynn than she's letting on?"

"She never got involved in my dating life before, even if she didn't like a woman I was seeing. She's only ever wanted me to be happy. Why wouldn't she like Saralynn?"

"I don't know, man. You're right. It doesn't make sense. She'll be at the arena all day tomorrow since it's a game night. Get her to talk. Looks like you both need it."

Madden nodded. This runaround had to stop. He'd like to get more than three hours of sleep a night. He hit the start button on his controller. "So, zombies?"

"Zombies."

Chapter Twenty-Three

At noon, Madden crossed the hall to Saralynn's office and knocked before poking his head in. "Hey, you up for lunch? I got takeout. Thought maybe we could eat down by the ice. It was just resurfaced after practice, so it has that crisp, fresh smell. Plus the lights are low, no one's around. A nice, romantic atmosphere." The perfect place for the conversation he wanted to have.

"Uh … " Her gaze swept over her desk, her computer screen, then the rest of the room like she was looking for something. Her posture was rigid, but she might've just been stressed about trying out the hockey stuff with the dance team tonight. Still. It was enough to take the edge off his appetite. Finally, she met his eyes. "Sure. I guess I can do a quick lunch. I have a lot to get ready for, though, so—"

"Quick it is." He held her door open with one hand, two bags of takeout in the other, while she grabbed her purse then started for the elevator. She kept a step ahead, but the hallway was narrow, so that didn't necessarily mean anything. The silent ride to the main concourse level was a little more disconcerting. Saralynn was not known for being quiet. And while she didn't back into a corner, she kept about a foot between them, painfully noticeable in the small space.

Before he could think of something to say, the door slid open, and she didn't exactly bolt, but it was not a slow exit. She led the way down into the stadium and didn't stop until she chose a seat right against the glass by the penalty boxes. He sat beside her and handed her a bag. Tried a smile.

"You really are in a hurry."

She'd already dug into her fries but looked up at him and returned the smile with a small sigh that drained most of the tension from her body. "Sorry. Tonight's a big night, and there's so much to do."

"Well, I have an idea that might improve your mood."

She smirked and kicked his shoe, just a tap, not enough to hurt. "You said a quick lunch. That'll add at least another fifteen minutes."

He laughed, and the tightness in his chest eased some. "That's not what I meant."

"Oh. Then I'm listening."

"Now I'm thinking about sex."

"Madden."

"Just kidding." Sort of. "Well, I had a long talk with Cole last night. Just between us, Tricia broke up with him, and he's not taking it well."

"Oh no." She frowned and paused with the cheeseburger halfway to her mouth.

"Yeah. He was in bad shape. He wanted to move in with her. I really feel for him. I've been there more times than I'd like to admit. But it got me thinking … maybe we should give it a shot."

It could've just been the blue glow from the rink's advertisement screens, but she looked paler. "Give what a shot?"

"Living together. We don't have to hide anything now. It would give us more time with each other, and I can think of numerous other benefits." He wiggled his brows.

All expression fell off her face, and the cheeseburger landed in the bag in her lap. "I … I don't think so."

"Why not?"

"I just got my apartment and decorated it. It took me three months to finish moving in, but I did, and it's my space. The first home that's just mine. I worked hard for it. And you've still got

Cole for a roommate. I'm not ready. Can't we just keep going like we've been?"

"We could … but I'm starting to get the feeling you'll never be ready."

"That's not fair. You said you'd be patient."

He had. And he wanted to be. But he'd made a bad habit of taking the passenger seat in relationships, and they'd never ended well. He just wanted to be copilots, but one sign after another was pointing to Saralynn never giving up the wheel. "Be honest. How far do you see us going?"

She stared at him, lips parted, and shook her head. "Why are you doing this? Why are you pushing so hard?"

Why *was* he? Was it because he really did believe in what they had and just wanted to be with her? Or was it because having a stable, solid relationship would show his sister he was ready and able to be a positive influence? As much as he wanted to deny the latter, he wasn't completely sure. "So you're saying no?"

"I'm saying not now."

"All right." He set his untouched bag of food by her feet and stood.

"Madden … "

He shook his head and climbed the steps, kept going even though he could feel her staring at his back. Whatever his motives were, he knew in his gut that they could wait six months, a whole year, and Saralynn would never be ready to take the next step, even if the next step was just trading keys. They weren't on the same page. Not even in the same book. And it felt like they never would be.

Chapter Twenty-Four

Friday Night, Surrender Nightclub

Vaughn Manor felt too big on a regular night, but it was unbearable now, and he was in no mood to be at the game. His presence wasn't required, and it was unlikely anyone would even know he was missing. Maybe Jace because they usually watched together. Then again, she might be glad for his absence. That thought stung, which was saying a lot because he couldn't feel very much at the moment. Not with five beers and three shots in him.

The alcohol and the Friday night crowd at Surrender kept him from thinking too deeply about anything. Add in the strobe lights and pounding music, and it was the best anesthetic he could hope for. A small voice in his head said this was a bad idea. He was supposed to be staying *out* of trouble, and getting this drunk rarely had a happy ending. That voice, however, was silenced by another shot he accepted from a passing server.

He took an open spot on the winding, plush, yellow sofa that spanned the room and let the chaos absorb him. A girl in a gold bikini swung around a pole on the platform behind him, and he glanced back just to make sure he wasn't going to get a go-go boot in the head.

He'd spent a lot of time working on himself the past two years after getting in deep with a loan shark. As far as he thought he'd come, it was depressing as hell to accept he had so far left to go. He'd gone into work that morning hopeful and sure of his reasons for wanting Saralynn to move in. But with dumbfounded and horrified way she'd stared at him, he might as well have proposed. After everything they'd gone through, he should have known how she'd react. He just couldn't resist. Once again, he dove into the ocean without checking for an undertow. But it wasn't all him. She'd started distancing herself the second he opened her door.

Some guy dropped down next to him and squinted. "Yo. Aren't you that guy who works for the Sinners? Vaughn? Your sister owns the team, right?"

Madden nodded but didn't make eye contact, didn't engage.

"Whoa. Awesome. Nice to meet you man, I'm Joe." He held out his hand.

Walking away wasn't an immediate option. He wasn't sure he could stand with the room tilting side to side like it was. He shook briefly and hoped Joe would get the hint.

He didn't. "I'm a big fan. I know the team's on the longest winning streak they've ever had, but the Stars have also been on a streak. What do you think? Can the Sinners pull out another one?"

It could go either way, but with the captain's head out of the game, another win was unlikely. He shook his head. "Not tonight."

"What's up with Cole? I was watching pregame warm-ups at a bar down the street, and he's not looking good. I mean like he wouldn't even make the minor league. He was taking shots on net, and he couldn't have hit the puck with a tennis racket."

"Lay off, man. How well would *you* play if your girl just broke up with you?"

"No shit? Guess that explains it. So you think they're definitely going to lose?"

"I don't know, but I wouldn't put money on a win."

"Thanks, man." Joe clapped him on the shoulder, stood, and disappeared in the sea of sparkly, half-naked people.

Madden frowned. Why would the guy thank him? Something nudged his brain, an obvious answer clouded by the beer haze. No more. He flagged down a server and tipped her twenty for a glass of water and to keep them coming. A half hour and a few bathroom breaks later, the nudge in his brain turned into a rock in his stomach.

He pushed his way out of the club and waited on the sidewalk for a taxi. No need to call one when they cruised the Strip twenty-four seven looking for tourist fares. The throbbing in his skull lowered to a manageable level. He pressed his palm into his forehead, and between that and the soft breeze, he was mostly sure he wouldn't throw up. That was subject to change, of course.

He still wasn't firm on the details, but instinct told him to call Saralynn. She needed to know about whatever was going on. She wouldn't be happy to hear from him, but she was the only one he trusted to sort it out. He dug in his pocket for his phone, scrolled through the log, and hit dial. It rang six times, and he expected voicemail, but she picked up and yelled over the deafening background noise.

"Madden? Hold on!" The roar of the arena gradually faded until the only sound was her ragged breath. "Where are you? What's going on?"

"I'm leaving Surrender."

"Are you drunk?"

He paused, probably too long. "Not anymore." She didn't respond to that. When a woman chewed you out, she was angry. When she didn't say a word, she was furious. He closed his eyes and forged ahead. "I think I messed up."

Chapter Twenty-Five

Las Vegas Arena

Normally on game nights, nothing could steal Saralynn's focus, especially when they were debuting a promotion, but all she could think about was Madden. How could he be so careless? She should have predicted this. He'd been so upset that afternoon. Yes, he pushed when he said he wouldn't, but if she were being honest, she'd started mentally backing away days ago. He sensed that, and while it was pretty clear he had his own stuff going on, she wasn't entirely blameless.

He hadn't answered a text or call all day. And when he finally got back to her, it was to report a potential disaster? A nagging feeling in her gut said to track him down and be his life preserver until he could keep his own head above water, but that wasn't an option. Any number of the hundreds on staff could miss a game and go unnoticed. She was not one of them.

And in any case, what could she do? Even if he were currently sober—big if since he'd still been slurring words—he'd admitted to drinking. Maybe he'd imagined the whole thing. Yeah. And maybe her brother would leave hockey for Disney On Ice. The Sinners could win. That would take some heat off if anything came of it. No time to think about it now.

She ran down the steps, her heels echoing. The elevator might have been faster, but maybe not, and she couldn't stand to get inside with the afternoon's silent ride still replaying there, a phantom reminder of one more memory she wished she could rewrite. At basement level, she burst out and jogged down the hallway. Right outside the locker room, in the space the guys used for pregame soccer exercises, the dance team shot pucks back and forth, staying in formation for the most part.

"Hey, ladies."

They looked up and beamed at her. Miranda, the captain, waved. "Hey, Sare. With only four days' practice, we're lookin' good. I think Coach Windham would be impressed."

"That's what I like to hear. The first period's almost over, and we're going to start with the three-on-three. The shootout will be after the second period. Everybody clear on what they need to do? Any questions?"

They all stared at her and shook their heads, looking a little like traumatized soldiers after war. Their war had been on ice every afternoon that week, their commanding officer Nealy the tiny tyrant. Saralynn had watched the first two practices, but they'd been so brutal, she couldn't bear to witness the rest. The women had started out with a rudimentary knowledge of how the game worked, which was nowhere near Nealy's standards. There had been strong words and tears, but it looked as if everything turned out okay in the end.

"Okay, great. Let's head around and use the ground floor B entrance to the ice. We don't want to go through the locker room and risk running into the guys. The littlest things psych them out, and they're already down by two. If they break their winning streak tonight, it won't be because of *us*."

Most nodded their heads. Superstition was nothing to mess around with. Saralynn waved an arm and led the march. By the time they got to the Zamboni entrance, the first period was over, and the players were heading off. The dance team laced up their skates and wobbled toward the ice. *Please don't let them fall. Please don't let them fall.*

That's all she needed—this honest effort to morph into a parody. One slip, and her mailbox would flood with complaints about the "bimbo cheerleaders" turning the game into a joke. At least they looked respectable in the blinged-out, signature Sinners' women's jerseys and yoga pants. She held her breath as they made their entrance. Their arms shot out for balance the first few steps, but nobody tumbled as they skated into place center ice. *Thank God.*

Six women took sticks while the other half sat on the players' bench. A ref skated out to drop the puck. And the arena went crazy. Normally, people left for bathroom or snack breaks, but the majority stayed in their seats to watch the real, live Barbie dolls play hockey. And the most surprising thing? They were *good.* They darted and dodged over the ice, passing, receiving, and stealing the puck cleanly. Even the line changes went smoothly as if they'd been doing this all season. Anyone who doubted the coaching magic of Nealy Windham wasn't paying attention.

And even with this unqualified success, she couldn't get Madden off her mind. Where was he now? He'd said he was going home, but in his state, it would be easy to get sucked into a shiny casino on the way. He normally spent games against the glass by the players' entrance with Jacey. She now stood there alone, and his absence was palpable.

The urge to fix everything overwhelmed Saralynn. That was her job and coded in her DNA. But she was torn between sympathy and frustration. How could you help someone who kept making things worse? He was a grown man. He could take care of himself. *Please, God, let him take care of himself. At least until tomorrow.*

The ref blew his whistle to end the dancers' game, and the crowed cheered as if the Sinners had been out there. Jacey caught her eye from the other end of the rink and nodded with two thumbs up. Boyfriend alarm bells aside—assuming she could still call him that—satisfaction swelled through her. If the dancers could make it through the mini game, the shootout would be no problem.

They skated off-ice waving to the audience, and she opened the rink door for them. One after another, they hugged her and whooped.

"That was awesome! I never knew hockey could be so much fun! I mean, it's exciting to watch, but to really go out and play? Can we do this every game?" Excitement rolled off Miranda in waves that practically shimmered around her, and Saralynn laughed despite herself.

"Not every game, but at least once every home stand. You guys were incredible out there."

"All thanks to Coach Windham. I'll be honest—she scared the Spanx off us the first day, but she knows what she's talking about."

"Well nice job, ladies. Stretch it out, get some water, and get ready for the second period break."

Their excited conversations echoed down the hall until the dim background noise of the arena took over, leaving Saralynn with her thoughts. *He's fine. He'll be fine.* She moved aside for the Zambonis to get through but stayed close to the glass. Everyone in the press box was taken care of, and she had a walkie-talkie if anyone needed her.

The overhead lights went down so only the advertisement screens glowed, casting a blue tint over the whole rink. She closed her eyes and inhaled deeply, the clean scent of fresh ice bringing her back to Reese's bantam days. The whole family would take up a first row bench and cheer him on. Shiloh and Sophie were actually nice to her. She was only five, but that's when she'd fallen in love with the game. When was the last time she'd really watched?

The Zambonis rolled off, and the officials reset the goal posts in their holes before the players returned. The Sinners were on her end of the ice this period, so she got a close-up view of her brother going through his rituals. He glided side to side in the crease, making traction marks exactly eleven times, hit his stick against each goal post as if crossing himself, then dropped into his game-on crouch. She smiled. Nice to know some things never changed.

The good vibrations stopped shortly after the horn sounded and the puck dropped. Within the first five minutes, the Sinners were down by another point, and it didn't look like it would get better. *Come on, Cole. Don't let Madden be right.* He was missing passes and shots on net. That never happened. Normally, Nealy would be screaming from behind the bench, but she just stood there, arms folded, face serious. That might be worse. Were they really going to lose for the first time in more than a month? If Bar Guy existed, he was about to make a lot of money.

And she'd have to clean it up.

Chapter Twenty-Six

Saturday, March 29th

I think I messed up.

The words kept repeating in her brain, making her more and more irate. Last night, she couldn't even strategize because she couldn't be sure "Joe" would say anything. She wasn't about to inform the media the Sinners' assistant GM advised someone to bet against his own team just so she could get ahead of a shitstorm that might never make landfall.

Except—of course—it did.

By mid Saturday morning, the news reports had spread through the Internet like wildfire. Apparently Joe had won big betting against the Sinners, and he thanked Madden for it. Loudly. So now it was all hands on deck, and she had to talk to the one person she didn't want to deal with even more than Madden.

She allowed herself one long, silent scream, put her television on mute, and reached for her cell.

Jacey answered on the first ring. "I hope you have a plan because I'm officially out."

Fantastic. "I just saw the news." It wouldn't help anybody to let on that Jacey's brother had spilled his guts the night before. "This guy could be making everything up for his five minutes of fame." Why was she still protecting Madden? He'd done this to himself. She'd messed up a lot, too, but one thing that had become clear in her time with the Sinners was the power of personal responsibility. If you didn't go looking for trouble, it had a harder time finding you.

"He's not making it up. I talked to Cole, and he said no one knew about his breakup but Madden. I can't believe he'd do that." Except there wasn't disbelief in Jacey's tone. She sounded angry, disappointed, and resigned. But not surprised. "Forget for a minute that he publicly told a stranger to bet *against* his own team. He betrayed his best friend. What's happening to him?"

Saralynn didn't have an answer for that. Madden was breaking down and making bad choices. The gambling rumor had had a domino effect. Jacey played a part, though it was hard to say how big, but no one could deny his culpability. Not anymore.

"Let's fix what we can fix. I'll release a press statement tomorrow saying that Madden didn't advise anyone to do anything. The man simply asked him what was going on with Cole, and Madden told him. This'll blow over."

And it would. News moved fast. The sharks would chew on this for a day or two, and then the next scandal would come along. Gossip wasn't the problem.

"That'll be fine. I trust your judgment."

It was undeserved. Her judgment hadn't been stellar lately. Had she held back in the relationship because part of her had seen this coming? From the beginning, she'd known Madden was a wild card. Unpredictable and lost. She'd known getting involved with him was a risk.

There had been a glimmer of hope, a glimpse of who he could be, but good intentions didn't define people. Actions did. And she'd worked too hard to let anything get in the way of her progress. If he was so gung-ho on sinking his own ship, she didn't have to go down with him. She had to do what was right for herself, and this time it wasn't selfish. It wasn't.

That didn't make it hurt any less.

Chapter Twenty-Seven

Vaughn Manor

The sound of heavy objects hitting the floor pulled Madden from deep sleep, but waking up didn't mean being completely aware. Not with a massive headache and what could only be a stomach full of battery acid. He rolled over on the couch and tried to remember. Surrender. The random conversation. Taxi home. Too many stairs to climb before crashing, so he'd ended up in the living room. That pattern needed to stop. His vision focused enough to see shapes. Those heavy objects were boxes landing on the foyer tile, flying in from the stairway to the second floor.

He stood with exaggerated slowness. The room didn't spin, and the carpet didn't sink like quicksand. Careful steps got him to the edge of the tile, where a heat-seeking hockey stick almost decapitated him. He ducked and just missed the follow-up duffle bag.

Cole stood at the top of the steps, chucking things down. "Move."

"Hey. What are you doing?"

"I'm leaving. You can't tell?" He threw down another box that landed with a thump heavy enough to make the crystals shake on the chandelier above them.

"You're … what?"

"Didn't expect me to stay, did you? After you tell some guy my personal business and suggest he bet against our team because I can't hack it with a fucking broken heart?"

Oh God. The previous night came back in clearer pieces, and it started adding up. That guy—Joe—thanked him because he was going to go place a bet. A bet that panned out. He must have gone to the press about it. That's what his subconscious had been trying to warn him about.

"Cole, I'm sorry. Seriously. I didn't mean to. I had a really bad day and a lot of beers and—"

"Save it. I thought we were friends, but I guess you really can't trust anybody."

"Please. Hold up for a minute. I know I screwed up, but if you could just let me explain."

"You know what, Mad? I've listened to you explain a lot of things. I never judged you, and I never repeated what you told me to anyone. You couldn't do the same for me just once. I'm staying at Colly's until I find a place. I can't deal with this now." He swept an arm in the direction of the boxes. "I'll be back for it." He shouldered the duffle, grabbed the hockey stick, and threw open the front door, then slammed it behind him.

Madden stood there, staring. Not even the hangover was worse than the self-resentment. Jacey was right. He broke everything. Confidences, trusts, friendships. But he could fix them too. He could. And he would. He had to.

Chapter Twenty-Eight

Sunday, March 30th

The old Saralynn wouldn't have blinked at breaking up with a man, and she'd almost never done it in person. She'd gone through it so many times, a memorized speech waited at the ready. She could recite it in her sleep. The problem was none of it applied this time. *I've had a really good time with you, but I don't think this is working out. We're in different places. Going different directions. We want different things. I met someone else. I'm not at a point in my life where I can be in a relationship.*

She couldn't say any of that to him. Their relationship *had* been working out. They'd been in the same place, going the same direction, and more or less wanting the same thing. She'd really thought she was ready to open herself up and really *be* with someone. Not just floating on the periphery waiting for an escape, but waist-deep, face to face in the confusing, complicated, messy, wonderful, and real middle of a relationship. But maybe she wasn't.

Pulling up his driveway, she fought the paralyzing urge to turn back. She needed closure, and he deserved it, if nothing else, from her. The towering home had felt inviting before, but now it was intimidating. Before she could think twice, she jogged up the steps and rang the bell. It echoed through the house, but there was no other sound. Not even footsteps. She knocked. No answer. He had to be there. His car was.

She tried the knob, and it turned in her hand. The door swung open but hit something. She pushed, and it moved slowly then stopped. Boxes?

"Madden?" A groan came from the living room. She wiggled inside and closed the door behind her, then hopped over the sea of cardboard until she hit carpet.

Madden sat on the couch in sweatpants and an old band T-shirt, staring at a TV on mute. After a minute, he switched it off and looked at her. "Hey."

That's all he had to say? She licked her lips, winding up for a lecture, but the boxes remained in her side vision. "What happened?"

He hesitated before responding. "Cole moved out." His voice was flat on the surface, but an undertone of sadness rippled through.

She lost a little steam. An echo of his pain touched her, but she pushed it down. "I'm sorry. But do you blame him?"

"No. I blame myself. I really screwed up." This might be what remorse looked like on Madden, but it was hard to tell. Despite his blank exterior, he seemed fragile. On the edge of falling apart. But she couldn't get sucked in.

"I don't exactly know what's going on inside your head. I can only guess. I know I'm not blameless. I'm confusing and contradictory, and most of the time I don't understand myself. But at some point, you have to own your choices. You care now, but why didn't you care Friday night as you were choosing to torpedo your life from bad to worse?"

He held her gaze, and turmoil churned in his stormy gray-blue eyes, but he didn't say anything.

"I thought you were past that pitfall. I took a chance on you because you said you were trying to be better. We had that in common. But I'm still trying every day, and you … it's like you've given up. I want to be there for you, but I don't think I can."

He stood and swayed toward her but didn't take a step, like he was afraid she'd leave. "I know I made a mistake. And I don't have a good excuse. At the time, I didn't think I *could* make things worse. I just wanted to stop the gnawing in my gut. I wanted to go numb just for one night. Cole is my best friend. The last thing I wanted to do was hurt him. It kills me that I did, but I didn't mean to. And Jacey … she's pregnant, and she doesn't know if she wants me around her kid. I am losing everyone I care about. Please. I don't want to lose you, too."

The raw heartbreak in his face almost stole her reserve. How long had he known about Jacey and not said anything? Was that why he'd been acting so manic? Hot tears slid down her cheeks, and her lips trembled. "I'm sorry. I really am. But I can *barely* keep myself on track. If I'm going to let people influence my life, it needs to be positive."

He leaned back like she'd slapped him.

She shook her head. "I didn't mean … look. I know you'll recover from this. You'll straighten yourself out and right the wrongs. I just don't think I'm strong enough to be your crutch right now."

I'm a terrible person.

He stood there, arms at his sides but hands open like he had to fight not to reach out for her. "Saralynn … "

"I'm so sorry, Mad." She wiped her eyes even as more tears fell and moved for the door as fast as she could, but he didn't follow her. Somehow that made it hurt even more. She didn't stop until she was in her car. Her hand shook as she buckled up, and it took three tries. When it finally clicked, she stared at the steering wheel, and the dam broke. Squealing whimpers escalated to sobs, and she held her face in her hands.

Was it true? Did she really need to break up with him to take care of herself? Or was she just being a selfish coward? Either way, remorse nearly ate her alive for the pain she'd seen in his eyes. Hadn't she warned him? Reese was right after all. She was relationship napalm. All the progress she'd thought she made, what if it wasn't real? The thought paralyzed her until she couldn't breathe, or maybe she was just crying that hard. She pushed her key in the ignition and took a shaky, deep breath, trying to pull herself together. It would get better. It had to.

Chapter Twenty-Nine

Tuesday, April 1st

Saralynn couldn't remember a single time she'd stared at the clock on her office computer, waiting for her lunch hour, but there was a first for everything. She almost hadn't made it out of bed on Monday let alone come into work, but Madden hadn't been there. He wasn't there today either. *It's my fault.* A knock on the door spiked her heart rate, but it was just her brother. In one of his game day suits.

"Hey. I'm here to take you to lunch."

She looked at the date on her day planner and frowned. "If this is an April Fool's joke, I'm not in the mood. I heard what you guys did to Colly, filling his car with packing peanuts."

Reese started to grin but studied her face and obviously thought better of it. "No joke."

"Is this because I melted down on the phone last night with Allie? I guess she told you."

"She passed on the bullet points, but this was my idea. Thought it was time for a root beer float."

Her eyes watered, and she blinked fast to keep from ruining her makeup. Again. When they were kids, any time something went wrong, from scraped knees to broken hearts, they'd have root beer floats. Kind of a Reese family cure-all. They hadn't done it since before he was drafted. She touched the back of her hand to her nose as extra precaution against the tears. "Wait a minute. You're not playing tonight. Why are you wearing a suit to take me for a root beer float?"

"Michael Mina's at the Bellagio. Best floats in Vegas."

That chipped a crack in her professional veneer that spread surprisingly fast, pushing her out of her chair and into Reese's waiting hug. He kissed the top of her head and patted her back. "I'm so sorry, Sare."

That was it. No *I told you so* or *This is what I was worried about.* No judgment at all. He'd dressed up on a random Tuesday just to take her out to a fancy lunch because he knew she needed it. Her brother was growing too. She still fought to hold in the ugly cry, but a few renegade tears escaped anyway.

Reese leaned back, pulled out his pocket square, and dabbed them dry. "Come on. We can talk there or in the car, whatever you want."

"Don't tell Allie, but you're still my favorite."

"There was ever a doubt?"

"Well, she is pretty awesome. It's been a close race."

"Can't argue with that." He slung an arm around her shoulders and led them out. It had been a while since she'd *looked* at the city. On her drives to and from the arena, she passed a lot of the same sights—all the big, shiny buildings and over-the-top colorful signs—but never saw them, always thinking about what she needed to do that day or the next. It really was beautiful, even during the day.

When they pulled up to the Bellagio, Reese handed off the keys to a valet and offered her his arm. She rolled her eyes at him but took it anyway. Michael Mina's wasn't very busy at noon midweek. It was too expensive for most business people who lived in Vegas and too formal for tourists, who spent their days in bikinis and flip-flops. Good. She didn't feel like being in a big crowd.

They sat at a small table by the window with a white, linen tablecloth and polished silver. Hard to believe this place had something as simple and plebeian as root beer floats. She scanned the menu for something to eat even though she hadn't been hungry since Sunday. When the waiter stopped by, she poked her head up. "I'll have the artichoke salad."

"I'll take the Chilean sea bass. And we'll both have root beer floats with the chocolate chip cookies."

The waiter had his mouth open, but they hadn't let him get a word in, and if he was intending to ask them which wine they preferred, he hid his surprise well at the float request. He simply jotted it down and nodded. "Very good. I'll bring some water and bread as well."

When he left, Reese was careful to keep his gaze directed out the window at the fountain bubbling in the courtyard, but his silence was as loud as a hundred questions.

Saralynn rearranged her silverware. "So I guess you want to know the details."

"If you want to tell me. You don't have to."

She scoffed. "Since when? What happened to the overprotective brother who warned a whole arena of men away from me?"

"That guy's still there. I just have a better idea of how to keep a grip on him now that I have a highly evolved and enlightened wife who helped me see the error of my ways."

"She improved your vocabulary, too."

He made a bucktoothed beaver face to show how funny he thought that was, but it backfired because it made her laugh.

"Sorry. Well, you know what happened with him Friday night."

He nodded. Everyone knew.

"Did you know Jacey's pregnant?"

"Carter told me, but I'm supposed to keep it on the down low until they're ready to announce. I don't think the world is ready for a mini-Phlynn."

Saralynn scrunched her nose at him. "Beside the point. Anyway, Jacey told Madden she wasn't sure she wanted him in the baby's life. I don't know when, but I get the feeling he's been carrying this a while. It would explain some things. But, as you probably

155

heard from Allie, Friday afternoon Madden asked me to move in. I said I wasn't ready, and he said he thought I'd never be ready. I'll admit, my own issues were at work, but he handled it so badly. And yeah, I've paid my dues to the bad decisions club, but I know better now. He seemed to be spiraling. So I went over Sunday and broke things off. Allie says I create my own hurdles."

"Getting in your own way is a Reese family trait. My wife can vouch for that."

"Am I heartless? Did I do the wrong thing?" What if she wasn't holding Madden at arm's length because he was the wrong guy? What if she was doing it because he could be the right one? The waiter dropped off the bread and their ice waters. She took a cold, fortifying sip.

"You're not heartless. You did a good job pretending for the first twenty-one years of your life, but I always knew there was a side you didn't let people see. Now you let it out, and I am so proud of you, Sare. Only you know if you did the wrong thing. But I notice you didn't ask me if you did the right thing."

He *had* been hanging around Allie a lot. He was starting to speak in her wise riddles that sounded like they contained an answer but refused to divulge it. "You think if I was sure I did the right thing, I wouldn't ask?"

"I think you're worried you made a mistake. I know I'm still catching up on it all, but from what I've seen, he means an awful lot to you. That urge to push him away is probably just fear of letting him in. And you mean a lot to him. He was clear about that when he came to talk to me."

"I know." Of all the things she doubted, Madden's feelings weren't one of them. That only fed her confusion. "And I do care about him. More than any guy I've ever dated. I just don't want to make any more mistakes. I'm afraid. I'm afraid of giving in and letting myself ... " *Love him.* The last two words didn't make it out but echoed in her head. Did she love him? Did she know what love was?

"You can't control or predict a relationship. That only worked in the past because you weren't invested. I know you're scared, but you already took the jump."

It was still terrifying. "You think I should give him another chance."

"I'm not saying that. I like Madden, and I think at his core, he's a good guy. But I don't know all his demons. There might be only two people in the world who do, and you're one of them. I'm saying don't write him off completely."

The waiter returned with their floats on a silver platter along with crispy, fresh chocolate chip cookies. "Enjoy. Your food should be right up." He bowed and turned on his heel.

"Are those dark and white chocolate straws?"

Reese smirked and took a long sip from his then sighed. "Didn't I say best floats in Vegas?"

She dug into the foaming ice cream on top with her spoon and closed her eyes in bliss as the cold, creamy vanilla hit her tongue. She might not know what to do about Madden, but the brother-sister time gave her the courage and determination to figure it out.

Chapter Thirty

It'd been a rough couple of days, and all that soul-searching hadn't led to any answers. After Saralynn walked out on Sunday, Jacey had called and left a message. He was suspended for the week while she figured out what to do. She didn't say it outright, but his job was on thin ice. And his place in her life. Everything he cared about was crumbling away, and he had to get out of the house. Be around people even if he wasn't with anyone.

He'd taken a taxi downtown with no real destination in mind, and he walked the Strip as the city came to life. One by one, the neon signs turned on, and they could usually foster some kind of pleasant feeling, but now they just reminded him of surprising Saralynn at the Boneyard. He moved forward in a stream of people, but it felt lonelier than being in the giant house by himself. All around him, couples held hands and families rushed to make a show time.

The next thing he knew, he was halfway in the door at Harrah's. He stopped and stared ahead at the blinking, flashing slot machines, heard dealers call at nearby tables. It almost felt like an invisible hand pushed on his back, trying to drive him inside to an easy escape, but that was an illusion. Losing himself for a few hours wasn't worth losing everything at the end of the night, even though he didn't have much left. He excused his way back out and checked his watch. Seven fifteen. Just enough time.

Another short cab ride took him to St. Thomas Catholic Church. Chairs were set up in a circle in the Sunday school room, and a few were still open. He took one and nodded to the group leader. He hadn't been to a meeting in a while, hadn't needed to.

The faces had almost entirely changed, but that was common, especially in Vegas. No shortage of gambling addicts here. It took some of the pressure off. A roomful of people who didn't know how much of a screw-up he could be sounded like just what he needed. No one looked at him in recognition, and the coil of anxiety in his stomach loosened a fraction.

"Okay, I'd like to call the meeting to order, if everyone could take a seat." The group leader leaned back in his chair and set an ankle on his knee. From Madden's experience, leaders always tried to look casual and relaxed and kept their posture open. It made people more comfortable, as if they were talking to a friend. Even though he understood how the psychology worked, the tactic was still effective. "Do we have anyone who'd like to go first?"

No one else raised their hand right away, so Madden did and got a nod as a go-ahead. "My name is Madden and I'm a compulsive gambler."

"Hi, Madden," echoed around the room.

"I've been gambling since my teens, and I've been through the program a few times, but I haven't gambled in two years." He waited for the quiet applause to fade before continuing. "Even though I haven't gambled recently, I'm starting to see how much my past gambling has affected my relationships and still does. My sister heard a rumor that I'd slipped up. She knows the truth now, but just that rumor made her question whether or not she wants me in my niece or nephew's life. She recently became pregnant."

Soft murmurs of sympathy surrounded him, and for the first time in almost a week, he didn't feel completely alone. These people understood better than anyone, and that connection, even if they were strangers, built him up. "I had too much to drink, and I said some things that hurt my best friend, and now he's not talking to me. My girlfriend broke up with me. And tonight I almost went in Harrah's. I could see the casino floor, and I *wanted* to gamble. Or I thought I did. But even then I knew, after years of hard experience, that it would hurt me in the end. So I came here."

More applause. The leader, Chuck, reached over and patted him on the shoulder. "I'm proud of you, Madden. We all know how hard that is. It took a lot of restraint and impressive insight. It's not easy to be strong in those moments."

"Thanks. I just wish I had been stronger last week. I went out for one drink, and it turned into five."

"It's common for gambling addicts to have other weaknesses, and alcohol addiction has a similar basis. We want to escape our problems and seek things that will allow us to do that. It's only when we realize we're compounding our problems that we can begin to better ourselves. It sounds to me like you've reached that place."

"I reached it two years ago, but I see now it takes effort to stay there. And I'm dedicated to that. I just wish I knew how to fix the damage I've done."

Chuck shrugged. "It's easy to forget the people we love don't owe us anything once we've broken their trust. We can only hope to earn it back through perseverance and listening to what they need from us."

Listening to what they needed. He'd been so caught up in wanting to explain his side, in defending or redeeming himself, that he hadn't absorbed what they were saying. Jacey was going through one of the biggest changes of her life, and she didn't do change well. Not without graphs, charts, and pro and con lists. Cole was everybody's secret-keeper but didn't trust his own secrets to many people. As young as he was, he didn't like to show weakness on or off the ice. Of course he felt betrayed. And Saralynn ... she'd told him at the beginning how hard she was trying to get herself together and that the road wouldn't be smooth. They all deserved more from him. Whatever it took, they'd get it.

Chapter Thirty-One

Saralynn stared hard at her open office door. It'd been a whole week, and Madden hadn't come to work. The urge to call him was almost more than she could take, except she still didn't know what to do, and part of her felt like she'd already done enough. Inflicted enough damage. Caused enough pain. But he'd been through a lot, and she needed to know he was okay. There was one person who might know, and that was a generous *might*.

Her boss's door was open, but she still knocked to announce her presence. Jacey glanced up, stress etched in her expression.

Saralynn closed the door but stood by it. This wouldn't be a comfortable, sit-down discussion. "Hi. I know you're busy, and this is probably the last thing you want to talk about, but I noticed Madden hasn't been at work all week. I'm not sure how much you heard—"

"Carter caught me up."

"Right." Easy to forget the six degrees or less of separation in this place. Carter and Reese had been best friends their whole lives. Naturally, Reese would tell him, and he'd tell his wife. "Well, I just wanted to see if you knew how he was doing."

Jacey stared at her for a long, uncomfortable moment. It was hard to decipher the emotions in her eyes, but none of them were happy. "I haven't spoken to him, but I left a message on his voicemail Sunday night. I suspended him for this week while I figured out what to do long-term."

Madden had messed up, but no one deserved to lose everything at once. "You haven't heard from him at all?"

Jacey's reserve cracked, and her voice betrayed it. "You probably think I'm cold or that I don't care about my brother. I love Madden. I've spent my life making sure he's okay. After our mother died, our father married his work. For a long time, it was Madden and me against the world. But he made a lot of promises he didn't keep. He became the boy who cried, 'It's different this time.' I kept believing him, and for a while that was fine. But it's not just me anymore. It's killing me to make these decisions."

The room shifted, and Saralynn leaned against the door. It wasn't hard to see how Jacey had come to feel the way she did. But more than ever, her heart ached for Madden. She had no doubt he'd been trying his best, and while she'd questioned a lot of things, his good heart had never been one of them. "I don't blame you for feeling that way. Everybody makes mistakes, and maybe he's made more than most, but I'd be lying if I said I wasn't in the same boat. Maybe he's still growing, but he *has* grown. He's facing consequences, and he's getting better. That has to be worth something. He deserves one more chance."

A little of the sadness left Jacey's eyes, and a small, shaky smile tugged at her mouth. "From you or me?"

"I can only speak for myself, but yeah, he deserves more from me. And I'm starting to think *I* deserve more from me." Saying it lifted an enormous load she'd been bearing the whole week. It felt good. It felt right. "Sorry. That probably didn't make sense."

"I think I got it. You know, Madden does have some good instincts. He was right about you."

"What do you mean?"

"He never told you?"

Curiosity sparked along with an anxious twinge. Saralynn shook her head. "Told me what?"

Jacey's smile took a firmer hold. "That is so Madden. We all liked you as an intern. You were hardworking and dedicated, and your idea for the Sinners' interactive mobile app showed true innovation and ambition. But when the spot for head of PR opened up, I had a list of candidates much more experienced. Madden campaigned hard for you, said he saw potential. I was on the fence, but he convinced me. I'm glad he did."

"Thank you, but I don't get it. Why wouldn't he tell me that?"

"My guess? He didn't want you to feel like you owed him anything."

A hundred other questions percolated. She couldn't decide what to ask first.

"I can only speculate. Whatever else you want to know, you should ask him."

"Okay. I will." She opened the door but paused. "He loves you. More than anything."

A new rush of tears gathered at the corners of Jacey's eyes. Her mouth pressed into a straight line as she fought them, and she nodded.

Saralynn eased out the door and closed it with a long exhale. If anyone understood the power of a second chance, she did.

Chapter Thirty-Two

Saturday, April 5th

Madden watched TV in the living room, a pizza on his lap and a can of A&W in his hand. After the meeting Wednesday night, he'd taken a couple days to himself. He hadn't completely hermited it, but a few trips to the grocery store and a couple interactions with delivery people had been the extent of his social interaction. Surprisingly, he felt a little better. The step back allowed for perspective.

When the doorbell rang, he put the TV on mute. Strange. He hadn't ordered anything else. Maybe Cole had come back to get the rest of his stuff. A rock formed in his abdomen as he navigated a path through the foyer. But it wasn't Cole. Saralynn stood on the front step in a clingy T-shirt, hot pink sweatpants that only reached her shins, and purple sneakers. Her big, dark eyes were uncertain and something else. His heart contracted with a painful hitch. God, he wanted to pull her close and never let go. But that wasn't up to him.

"Hey." She didn't say anything else. She didn't run away, either.

"Do you want to come in?"

"If that's okay."

"Yeah, please." He opened the door wider and waited until she'd climbed over a few boxes before closing it behind her. Hope flickered against his better judgment. She kept on walking into the living room and moved the pizza box aside to sit on the couch, so he followed.

"Embracing the bachelor life?" Her light teasing buoyed that hope, but he pushed it down.

"Not so much. It's not as grand as it seems. T-shirt and sweats is a good look on you. Very sexy." Not that he was a fashion template in nothing but basketball shorts. And truthfully, she could make a paper bag sexy.

She smiled, but it wavered. "I'm sorry—"

"No, *I'm* sorry—"

She touched a finger to his lips, effectively cutting him off and raising the crackling tension between them that sometimes hid in the background but always existed just below the surface. "I'm embarrassed to admit this, but apologies are kind of a new thing for me, so if I could just get it out all at once?"

He nodded.

"Thanks. I'm sorry about Sunday. I'm sorry that I ran away at the first challenge. I'm not defending what you did, but I think breaking up was more about me than you. I've never stuck around long enough in a relationship for a problem to even come up, let alone long enough to get through one. I've been working on me for the past year, and I realized that sticking with you through this wouldn't be a regression. Walking away from you would."

"Are you saying you want to be with me to break a pattern?"

"*No.* You are the reason I want to break my pattern. Let's be honest. I'm kind of stubborn."

A snort escaped before he could stop it, and for a second, it looked like she was going to hit him, but then she laughed.

"Yeah. Okay, really stubborn. The point is, no one can derail me but me. What I was really afraid of—what I *am* really afraid of—is letting someone in. But losing you scares me more."

So many emotions thrummed inside, he couldn't identify them all. "Losing you scares me, too." He leaned in, and she met him halfway. After the past week, the gentle brush of her lips almost broke him. He tentatively slid closer, and she cupped his face in her hands. The tenderness in that gesture almost brought him to tears. He wrapped his arms around her and deepened the kiss. A current of desire pulsed through him. He slid his hands through her hair, every atom in his body charged with light and need.

When he could think beyond the urge to touch her, he broke away just enough to look in her eyes. "I'll do anything to earn your trust back."

She stroked the back of his neck and nodded. "We can take it day by day." She kissed him again, and whether she believed him or not, the intensity of that kiss said she was willing to give him a chance, and that was good enough for now. He slid his hands up her sides and rolled his thumbs along the bottom curves of her breasts.

Her breath caught, and she climbed into his lap and arched into him like she couldn't get close enough. He knew the feeling. There were so many things he wanted to tell her. Not just that he was sorry, but everything he was sorry for. Everything he'd learned. Her fingers dug into his hair, and her hips rocked against his. Words could wait.

The need to truly be with her, to connect on the most primal level, was overwhelming. He stood, taking her with him, then set her down and held out his hand, asking without asking if this was what she really wanted. She slid her fingers into his palm and nodded.

He led them up the marble staircase and down the hall to his room. Faded sunlight revealed a small pile of clothes on the floor, but at least there wasn't anything else too embarrassing, like cartons of takeout or spoiled milk containers.

She took him by the shoulders and pushed him down on the edge of the bed, then slowly peeled off her T-shirt, revealing a silky bra. The sweats came off even slower. She was teasing him, making him ache, but it was worth it. Her thumbs dug under the elastic of her thong, revealed the tattoo on her hip, and he was a goner.

• • •

Saralynn had never been so nervous in her life, but the raw want in Madden's eyes gave it an exciting edge. A little strip tease wasn't new, but this was the first time she was baring more than her skin.

A little extra sway in her hips helped the sweatpants slide down, and she kicked them to the side. After unhooking her bra and letting it join the rest of her clothes, she stepped between his knees and tilted his head up for another kiss.

He gave it freely, his hunger and need making her knees weak. His hands skimmed her thighs and sides until his thumbs slid under the curves of her breasts. She moaned softly against his lips, and he took the cue, sliding backward on the bed until she could join him. As soon as she stretched out over him, aligning every exquisite pressure point with every one of his, he rolled them and shed his shorts.

After a few frantic seconds of finding a condom in the nightstand, he settled between her legs and took his time sliding home. Even though she'd been more than ready, he still didn't rush it. The sweet torture nearly did her in before they could start. A trembling whisper was the most she could manage. "Please … "

He dipped his head and kissed her, closing the last distance between them. His slow, hard rhythm guaranteed she wouldn't last long, and she hooked her heels behind his knees, meeting every thrust. Every nerve in her body hummed with pleasure, but it went beyond that. He raised her arms above her head and laced his fingers through hers, holding them there. They were joined on every level, and she let him in.

He picked up the pace but held onto her hands, rocking into her with escalating speed and strength until he lost himself with a deep moan, taking her with him. The sensation was so strong, his fingers threaded with hers was the only thing keeping her from splintering into a thousand, glowing pieces. His hips rolled against hers gently as they rode out the aftershocks, and she gradually came back to earth.

It felt like she was floating above her body. With him, in this moment, nothing could touch them. He rolled so they were on their sides, but they remained connected. "I can't even—"

"I know." She smiled and traced the lines of his face with her fingertips, over his cheekbone and down his strong jaw.

He kissed her nose. "I'm sorry for how I dealt with everything. That's not who I want to be."

"Why didn't you ever tell me you got me my job?"

"I needed to know if you'd go out with me because you wanted to. Not because you felt obligated. I didn't vouch for you expecting anything other than a good employee. You already fulfilled that."

She kissed him, soft and lingering. "You barely knew me when I applied."

"I knew enough. You were driven and creative. You wanted it more than anyone else. I had no doubt you'd be the best for the position. And you have been."

"I'd accuse you of sweet-talking, but we already had sex."

"God's honest truth."

"I believe you." She nuzzled his chin.

"Now if I can just figure out how to make it up to Cole. He won't talk to me."

"He'll talk to me. I know he's upset, and he has a right to be, but he's *Cole*." No need to explain that. Dylan Cole was one of the genuinely nicest people she'd ever met. He had a big heart. And that kind of guy couldn't write off his best friend so easily. "It'll be okay."

"What can I do for *you*?" He kissed her forehead.

She smiled and slid a hand down his chest. "I bet I can think of something."

Chapter Thirty-Three

Monday, April 7th

While she didn't have every hour of his day figured out, Saralynn could count on Dylan Cole to be in one place without fail at nine forty-five on the morning of a home game. She caught Madden's eye through his office window on her way to the elevator and winked. He was on the phone but nodded, not looking as confident as she felt. No matter what, she would get them in the same room.

The fastest way to the ice was to take the elevator to the basement and go through the locker room, but that wasn't an option. Practice had just let out, and ninety-nine percent of the team would be getting naked and hitting the showers, her brother among them. She shuddered and hit the button for the main concourse. It was kind of creepy this early, completely abandoned with the concession stands unlit. Compared to the glowing rush and bustle it would become later, it felt sad.

She took a set of steps down through the seats. At least the empty rink was filled with bright light. And one last hockey player. Cole glided from center ice toward the goal, working on his puck control. He circled behind the net then fired it in backhand. That might not have been impressive on its own, but he'd done it with his eyes closed. Only when she clapped did he look up, sweat pouring down his face. She walked around the front row to the railing that lined the tunnel exit, and he skated off-ice to meet her on the other side of it.

"Hey. Somethin' I can do for you?"

"Actually, yes."

"Why do I get the feeling it's a big favor?" He unhooked his helmet and took it off, tucking it under an arm. The dark spikes that weren't matted to his head poked up in different directions. He'd be downright adorable if it weren't for the hockey smell that could singe nose hairs.

"Because it might be the biggest."

He tilted his head back as understanding dawned in his eyes. "I know you're trying to help, but I don't have anything else to say to him. I was gonna have Colly stop by his place and get the rest of my stuff."

She sat on a concrete step and leaned her forearms on her knees. "You have every right to be upset. But you know him. He wouldn't do something like that to hurt you. You're his best friend. That night wasn't about you at all, even though you got dragged into it."

"What do you mean?" He leaned his stick against the glass.

"Earlier that day, he asked me to move in. It would take days chatting up Freud on a Ouija board to fully unpack my mental baggage, but I said no. And he's going through some serious stuff with his sister, but you should probably hear about that from him."

Cole's face went blank, then concern replaced his anger. "Shit."

"He knows he handled that night the wrong way, and he is *so* sorry."

"So why isn't he telling me all this?"

"He tried. You wouldn't let him."

Cole lowered his head for a minute, studying his skates. When he looked up, it was with playful suspicion. "Why are *you* telling me?"

She blanked at how quickly he'd shifted her to the hot seat. Her only response was a guilty smile. "When I got over wanting to tape his picture to a punching bag, I missed him. I realized my life was less without him in it. That's never happened to me. My brother might have told you stories."

Cole glanced away and shrugged.

"Uh-huh. Well, I've broken up with guys for every possible reason. Sometimes for no reason. But I never regretted it or doubted my decision."

"Until now."

"Yeah. Madden saw the best in me before I could even see it in myself. I think he does that for everyone. Will you at least talk to him?"

It took a few seconds, but Cole nodded. "I didn't want to believe he would do something like that just because. Besides. Colly snores like a moose. I can hear it from his couch."

She grinned. Ben Collier's dating life might hit a snag if that piece of information got out. Most likely it already had with Cole sleeping in his living room.

The captain picked up his stick and angled for the locker room.

"Oh, hey. I didn't get to say before, but I'm sorry. About Tricia. I know this doesn't mean anything now, but believe me when I say there's someone better out there who will realize you're a catch and appreciate that."

His face had fallen, but it brightened by the time she finished. "Thanks. It was hard. But I guess if she couldn't be okay with my schedule, it never would have worked out. It's not easy to find someone who understands you."

"I know exactly what you mean. You'll find her. Don't give up."

"Not in my DNA. And thanks, but my chances might improve if I take a shower. Guess I better ... " He gestured down the tunnel.

"Yeah. That might be a good idea."

He lifted a gloved hand in goodbye and ambled down the carpet to the locker room. Mission Break the Ice: complete. The rest was up to Madden.

Chapter Thirty-Four

"Dude, you have a rock collection or something?" Madden hefted a box that had to weigh thirty pounds and trudged up the marble staircase behind his best friend. On the surface, it was needling, but in man-speak, it meant *I'm glad you're back.*

"Those must be my pucks." Whatever Cole was carrying, he didn't struggle at all. Must've been clothes.

"Did you keep one from every game you ever played?"

"Just the benchmarks. Hat tricks, every time I hit 100 games, the Cup winners, stuff like that."

"Just the benchmarks" for Cole might as well have meant every game. When they got to the kid's room, Madden dropped the cargo with as much ceremony as he could manage. "I know I said it already, but I'm sorry. This place was really empty while you were gone."

"It's all right. We're cool."

"And I swear I'll never—"

"*Dude*, I know. Seriously, it's okay."

No matter how many times he apologized, it didn't feel like enough, even though Cole insisted otherwise. The self-inflicted guilt would take time to go away, and maybe that was a punishment on its own.

"Please say you ordered a pizza. Colly's a health freak. His fridge is full of celery and kale. His idea of junk food is low fat, non-dairy ice cream, which he eats once a month. I've been starving for more than a week. One night I broke down and ate McDonald's in my car. He accused me of fry breath as soon as I walked in."

Madden made a face. "That's no way to live."

"Tell me about it."

"Pizza's on its way. In the meantime, I have frozen hot wings we can stick in the oven."

Cole feigned a sob and wiped his dry eyes with a fist. "I'll never leave home again."

"Yeah, okay. Why don't you bring up the last couple boxes, and I'll throw the wings in?"

"I'd say you just want to get out of manual labor, but my stomach's about to digest itself."

"Done deal." And yes, he was happy to get out of box duty, especially since there was a weight set that hadn't made it back up yet. Cole could consider it cross-training. Win-win. He jogged into the kitchen and pulled out a baking sheet. One of the few kitchen basics he could find with his eyes closed. Before she left, Jace had organized everything to her OCD standard, and while he liked to cook from time to time, all he needed on a daily basis was a way to heat up frozen food. Dump and defrost.

As soon as he set the timer, the doorbell rang. The sound of a box dropping preceded Cole's disappointed, "You're not the pizza guy."

"Thank you for noticing. And making a girl feel welcome." Saralynn's voice boosted his heart rate.

When he joined them in the foyer, Cole had picked her up in a hug. She laughed and patted his shoulder. "Okay, okay. I'm sufficiently welcomed."

"You can put her down now."

Cole set her back on her feet, but not before kissing her cheek. He pointed at Madden. "*Now* we're even."

"So it's gonna be like that, huh?" He hoped there was no ire in his tone. The kid hadn't done any serious flirting even though Madden's gut tightened anyway at the display. Then Saralynn skipped over, took his face in her hands, and planted one square on his mouth. With heat. No mistaking her affiliations. When she rocked back on her heels, he winked at Cole. "Never mind. Wings in ten." He kissed Saralynn's nose. "Was there something you wanted to discuss … ?" *Preferably alone?*

"Yes, but Cole can sit in. In fact, he might have some ideas."

Well, there went hopes of naked time. "Oh. All right, well—" The doorbell chimed again. "That *will* be the pizza man, so how 'bout you guys go sit in the kitchen and I'll be there in a minute? And Cole? No more touchy."

"Whatever you say." He held his hands up in innocence and disappeared around the corner. Saralynn blew Madden a kiss then followed.

He dug in his pocket and pulled out a twenty. The pizza was only fifteen. He opened the door, took the box, and handed the man the folded bill. "Keep the change." Madden skidded into the kitchen, but the two of them were just sitting at the island, watching him with amusement. "Didn't want to let it get Cole. Cold. The pizza."

"Smooth, man."

Little brothers. Who was he kidding? It was still good to have Robin back at the Batcave. "Observations to yourself and get the wings out of the oven."

"On it." Cole jumped up and grabbed the insulated mitts off the counter.

"So." Madden set the pizza in the middle of the island and got three plates from the cupboard. "What are we brainstorming?"

Saralynn crossed her legs on the stool. In those fitted jeans, it took concentrated effort to pay attention to her response. "I want you to host Skates and Plates this year. We'll make a big deal about promoting it that way, and you can even serve with the rest of the team. I think it'd be a good chance to show your loyalty and dedication while at the same time showing there's no bad blood between you and the guys."

Skates and Plates was an annual charity event where the players dressed up in tuxes and served dinner to donors at the arena. He'd attended every year, but never as a waiter.

"Uh … " Cole set the sizzling sheet of wings on the counter. "I forgave him, but I'm not sure the rest of the team has."

Madden frowned. "I tried to talk to them, but they didn't want to hear it."

"I'll try my luck. And Cole, if you and Reese can vouch for Madden, I bet they'd listen."

"Worth a shot, but I can't make promises. They think Madden believes they can't win without my head in the game." Cole picked a few pieces of chicken up with his fingertips and dropped them onto his plate then piled on a tower of pizza.

"You're an integral part of the team and the best player in the league. But there's a lot of depth on every line, and I never meant for them to take it the way they did. Not that I can blame them." Madden sat next to Saralynn and took his own helping of fortifying comfort food. "Skates and Plates. You really think that'll work?"

"One way to find out." Not the most reassuring words in the world, but the confidence in her big, dark eyes made up the difference. Even with his doubts he trusted her instincts.

Chapter Thirty-Five

Saturday, April 12th

Madden straightened his bow tie then approached the next group in line. "Welcome to Skates and Plates; let me show you to your table. Can I have your last name?" He didn't even have to concentrate anymore. Those lines had burned into his brain over the past twenty minutes and came out on reflex now. That was good because a million other things occupied his thoughts, chiefly that the entire team *still* hadn't forgiven him.

It'd been a strong joint effort, but a few players wouldn't let it go. He'd felt like an ass for even asking. They deserved to be angry. The problem was, a couple of them weren't okay with turning this event into a public peace summit, and they'd been vocal about that. The truth was, it made him just as uncomfortable, but Saralynn had been so sure this was best for the team's overall image.

So here he was, ushering people to their seats, and in ten minutes, he'd give a welcome speech then start serving with the rest of the guys. The donors didn't appear to have any issues with him playing master of ceremonies. No disapproving looks or underlying hostility. There was enough of that from the handful of players who still considered him a traitor.

He sat three more groups at tables around the transformed rink before someone tugged on his elbow. Saralynn. Her long hair fell over her shoulders in silky, loose curls, and she wore a floor-length, black dress that hugged her slender body and sparkled under the arena lights. His runaway train of thought went off the rails, taking his entire vocabulary with it.

"Hey, handsome. You're up." She gave him a microphone and nodded toward the small stage.

Oh. Right. Benefit. He swallowed the lump in his throat then wound through the maze of tables and up the few steps to the podium. "Good evening. Ladies and gentlemen, I'd like to welcome you to the Las Vegas Sinners' annual Skates and Plates dinner and thank you for your generous donations to our youth hockey league." Polite applause echoed around the dressed up rink, easing some of his nerves.

"I'll be joining the team and coaching staff serving you tonight in our finest because I think this is a very worthy cause." It was true, but at the same time, it felt like lying. He'd be sitting at the head table with Jacey if Saralynn hadn't orchestrated all this as his comeback, and there was no shortage of guilt for that. "So sit back, relax, and enjoy the night. Thank you again." More applause, but music cued up in the middle of it, and everyone went back to their conversations. He stepped out of the spotlight and handed the mic off to one of the staff, then headed for the makeshift kitchen on the other side of the locker room.

A PR intern folded a cloth napkin over his arm and handed him a notepad and pen. "You have table twenty. Go ahead and take their drink orders, either red or white wine. There are pitchers of water already on the tables, so you just have to fill those glasses. Serve the wine and we'll go from there."

Simple enough. Saralynn's crew had every detail under control, but he expected nothing less. They learned from the best. All of the tables were numbered, and his was near the back. "How are you all? A pleasure to serve you tonight." He walked around carefully filling each water glass then took the wine orders. So far so good.

He felt a little better after delivering the salads. Everything was going smoothly and no complaints. Once he dropped off dinner orders to the cooks, there was nothing to do but wait. The locker room door opened, and Saralynn poked her head around. She met his gaze, winked, and mouthed "looking good." Maybe it would go off without a hitch after all.

• • •

It was working. It was really working. The crowd had responded well to Madden, and the mood of the room was light and positive. The past few days, Saralynn had been eating her nerves—translation: her body weight in M&M's—to cope with the stress. She'd tried to make it clear to holdouts like Ben Collier that even if they didn't accept Madden's amends, they'd be civil throughout the event and keep their opinions to themselves. Hockey players weren't known for that, hence the M&M's.

She'd checked on donors, servers, and staff. Technically, there was a spot for her at the head table, but she hadn't sat down all night. This was too important. Lacking an immediate task, she stood by the stage and kept an eye on the room.

One by one, players and coaches emerged from the tunnel carrying big trays. Finally, Madden appeared. God, he looked amazing in that tux. He put on a good show for the people at his table, but even from across the rink she could see worry in the lines of his face. He'd been uncomfortable shifting any attention to himself for the event. The only way she'd convinced him to go through with it was by proving that it would help the team. It wouldn't be good for anyone if the public thought there was dissension in the Sinners' ranks. They needed to gloss over the incident and move on as a united front. All of that was true, but deep down she was doing it for the man who'd reached her heart. The man who showed her she had one.

Madden was serving his last plate when he took a step back and bumped into Collier. Huh? Colly's table was on the other side of the room. She'd made sure of it. Madden turned around and apologized, but Colly pushed on his shoulder and sent him off balance. He fell into another player with a tray. It seemed like the food flew in slow motion and rained down on the guests. The responding shrieks caught everyone's attention. The music cut out.

Damn it. She hurried through the crowd and bent to check on the people wearing their dinners. "I'm so sorry. Is everyone okay? We'll get all of this cleaned and get you fresh entrees."

"You have some nerve, man." The intent in Colly's voice caught her attention.

She turned from the guests and slid between the two men, keeping her voice down and smile in place. "Ben, it was an accident."

"That's not what I was talking about."

"I'd like you to remember and respect our agreement for tonight. Could you do that for me?" She closed the distance and set a hand on his arm, snaring his gaze and trying to hold it, but he kept looking over her shoulder at Madden.

"He shouldn't be here. What kind of executive bets against his own team?"

"He didn't—" Before she could get another word out, Colly moved around her, knocking his shoulder hard against Madden's as he walked out. The whole room had watched the exchange, and from their expressions, heard it. The redness in Madden's face and the shame in his eyes broke her heart, but consoling would have to wait.

She headed for the stage as fast as she could and grabbed a mic from one of her staff. "Ladies and gentlemen, I'm so sorry for the disruption and hope you'll forgive us and enjoy the rest of the evening. We'll get everyone cleaned up and get new food out to you momentarily." But before she could even finish her sentence, the guests covered in chicken francese were gathering their coats and belongings. Operation Fix-It was going up in flames.

Chapter Thirty-Six

Monday, April 14th

I'm fired. I'm so fired. Saralynn sat at her desk, waiting for the call into Jacey's office. She'd tried to talk to Madden after the disastrous event, but he'd left as soon as she closed the night with thanks and one more apology. He hadn't answered his phone all day Sunday. She'd picked up her keys three times but never made it out the door. He'd obviously wanted to be alone.

So now her heart was trying to break the sound barrier not just in anticipation of the worst and most deserved disappointment speech she'd ever receive but also of facing Madden. They'd gotten so close, pushed beyond his insecurities and guilt, even made headway on hers, and it felt like all that progress just vanished. Needing space was never a good omen for a relationship. She had plenty of experience as the one requesting it. *I need to be on my own for a while. I need to figure things out.* They sounded reasonable on the outside, but what they really meant was *I can't do this.* It had taken twenty-three years to find this. Could she lose it so fast?

Her stomach lurched when Jacey's voice came through the intercom. "You can come in."

She took a deep breath through her nose and tried to keep her breakfast in her stomach. That breakfast might've only been coffee, but recycling it in her boss's office wouldn't help her case. She couldn't control what Madden would do, but she could do one last thing for him.

As soon as she let herself in and closed the door, she focused on Jacey. "Saturday night was not his fault. He had what turned out to be very valid reservations, but I chose to proceed with my plan. I should have picked up on the lingering tension with Collier and not pushed so hard to attach Madden to the event. I take full responsibility." From the corner of her eye, she could see Madden staring at her, incredulous.

"Saralynn, your idea was a good one. Had it turned out differently, it *would* have been good for the team. We all thought the guys could get along or at least fake it for one night, and most of them did. Collier's being fined and suspended for two games."

"Jace, no. The playoffs are starting, and—"

"Colly's an important part of the team. I know. But he just short of publicly attacked an executive and made a scene during a team event. I have to deal with that, and you know it."

"Let's be honest," Madden said. "I caused all this in one way or another, and I didn't mean to. I was just never a right fit for this position. I wanted to be a part of Dad's legacy, but under the envy, I always knew he was right to give it to you."

"Maddie … " Jacey's eyes watered, and she pressed her lips together until they were pale.

Madden's implications were clear, and as scary as that was, Saralynn had to fight the urge to slip out of the room. This was private between brother and sister, and this felt like intruding.

"I love you, sis. I want what's best for you. And for me. I don't think this is it." His throat worked as she assumed he was trying to keep his cool. "So I'm resigning as assistant GM. I'm gonna find something that suits me better. Just don't blame Saralynn for Saturday night. It was all me. Everything she's done since she started has helped the team. You need her."

He finally met her eyes, and the emotion there nearly undid her, too. *I need* you. She needed to say something, anything to slow things down, but her mind was completely blank. Of all the things she expected from Madden in this meeting, his resignation wasn't one of them.

Jacey seemed equally stunned, staring at her brother as if she'd never seen him before.

Madden looked at both of them. "You're probably getting tired of me saying it, but I'm sorry. For everything." He went out the door and kept walking.

For a second, Saralynn just stared after him in shock, then took off at a jog, ignoring the curious stares. She just made it in the elevator before the doors closed and grabbed his arm as soon as they did. "What the hell was that?"

"I meant what I said. I never fit here. The past couple months made me see what I'd been ignoring. I was good at my job, but it was never really what I wanted to do." It was the lack of fire in his voice, the calm, even tone that made her nervous.

"What are you gonna do?"

"Long-term, I don't know. Right now, I need to get away for a while. Figure things out."

The words nearly knocked her down. She set a hand on the railing and held it tightly enough that she wouldn't shake. All those guys she'd dated and dumped, had they felt like this? *What about me? What about us?* The questions threatened to burst out of her mouth without permission, but she held them in. If he had comforting answers, they wouldn't be having this conversation.

He reached out and took her free hand. "I'm not saying I want to—"

"Don't." She pulled her hand away and forced herself to meet his eyes as the doors opened to the basement hallway. "How about we don't say anything right now?"

He flinched, and God, it took every ounce of strength she had not to hug him and beg him to stay. He hesitated a second, then leaned down and kissed her briefly before walking off the elevator. She was too numb to follow him any farther. It wasn't until the doors closed that it hit her. They might be over. Really over. And she'd just let him go.

Tears fell faster and faster. She clamped a hand over her mouth and cried into it, afraid if she didn't, she'd scream instead. Before the elevator could move, she hit open. Madden was already gone, but she wasn't going after him.

She knocked on Allie's door and fell into her sister's arms.

Chapter Thirty-Seven

Monday, April 21st

Madden's feet sunk into the wet grass as he walked the grounds of Lake View Cemetery. A brisk wind made him hold his coat closed with one hand and carry the bouquet in his other, chin down and eyes up as he counted trees. It had been a few years since his father's burial, and he hadn't been back. Following landmarks was the best bet.

He'd spent one week in Cleveland. A lot colder than Vegas, and a hell of a lot grayer, but the familiar streets and buildings warmed him in a way that he'd missed. When you spent the first twenty-five years of your life in a place, it would take longer than a two-year hiatus to dissolve the feeling of *home* when you came back.

He'd stayed at the hotel connected to the old arena downtown. So much of his childhood echoed in that place. That's why he'd picked it. But instead of the expected comfort, it felt like hanging out with ghosts. Apparitions of his past lurked around every corner, reminding him of what was and would never be again. He'd switched to a Holiday Inn just outside the city limits after two nights and slept better.

It hadn't been his intent when he left Las Vegas, but after checking the local paper, he'd made some calls and went on a few accounting interviews that showed promise. The thought of working with numbers was appealing. He was a lot better at saving other people's money than his own. It would be a safe choice.

There it was. The old maple shading the Vaughn family plots. It was just starting to bud but remained mostly skeletal, adding to the eerie feel of the place. The cemetery was known for its ornate mausoleums and statues, so it wasn't a surprise their father had chosen it, but the raised stone Jack Vaughn shared with Madden's mother was relatively simple. Smooth, speckled pink marble, an angel in the middle, and engravings on either side. Cecelia Vaughn, loving wife and mother, gone too soon. He couldn't even remember her. Jonathan James Vaughn, devoted husband and father. Well, the first part was true.

Jacey had always said Jack had been a different person when their mother was alive. Lighthearted, funny, home. Madden had to take her word for it. In his memory, their father had been distracted, distant, away. They were always taken care of, though, and that was something. The Jack Vaughn he knew believed in committing yourself 100 percent to your goals and achieving them at all costs.

Madden laid the yellow roses over his parents' grave then pushed his hands in his pockets. No one was around mid-afternoon on a Friday, but still, it wasn't easy getting the words out. "Hey, Mom. Dad. It's been a while. You'd be so proud of Jace. She turned the team around and even won a few Cups. She got married, and you have a grandchild on the way. Me? I threatened pretty much all of that. So you were right, Dad. I wasn't ready for that kind of responsibility. But I'm doing better finally, and I'm trying to work it all out. If you've been watching, you know it hasn't been a straight road."

The confession felt good, liberating. As many times as he'd been through gambling programs, he'd never been able to complete this stage—apologizing to everyone he'd hurt or disappointed. When Jack Vaughn was living, an apology hadn't seemed warranted. After he died, it hadn't seemed possible. Or maybe that was an excuse. Apologizing to his father meant admitting he'd screwed up to the man who didn't understand or accept screw-ups. He'd spent the majority of his life trying to prove himself, but for what?

"I wanted to make you proud, Dad. But it was like no matter what I did, you didn't notice. It took me way too long to figure out I should be making myself proud. All that time spent trying not to let you down and I didn't think about how I was letting myself down. I don't know if that's the point you were trying to make or if you were even trying to make a point. I just know it's time to live my life for me. Not you or Mom, or even Jace. I'm not sure what that means yet, but I'll figure it out."

Just as the weight of twenty-seven years began to lift, he closed his eyes and saw Saralynn. They'd only dated for two months but they'd been through so much it felt longer. She hadn't said anything in the elevator, hadn't asked what would happen to them. Maybe she knew it was for the best. For both of them. He'd make a place for himself here, and she'd turn the Sinners into the top moneymaking team in the league. Jace would have to invent a new job title to promote her to. And Saralynn would find someone else. Someone who wouldn't constantly jeopardize her career. Someone who would put her first. That thought hit him like a punch. Did doing the right thing always hurt so much?

Chapter Thirty-Eight

Friday, April 25th

"Did he pout?" Saralynn took an armful of groceries from Allie and held the door open while her sister-in-law waddled inside, holding another big bag topped with two quarts of ice cream.

Allie set it on the kitchen counter and started unloading. "Yes, and it was adorable and heartbreaking. Your brother just wants to be there for you. But I explained to him that there are times when a girls' night is absolutely necessary."

God, that was true. Madden had been for gone two weeks, every day just as excruciating as the last. Not a single call or text. It was unforgivable. She'd spent equal time crying and railing at pictures of him on her phone. It was humiliating. After a breakup, she'd never given a guy more than a day's thought. This one was burned in her heart and not leaving any time soon. "Oh good. There's wine in my bag."

"Two bottles. In case you didn't want to share. And over here we have rocky road and mint chocolate chip as well as marshmallows, chocolate bars, and cheese puffs."

"We will be so sick. A decent distraction tactic. You're a good sister."

"For the record, this isn't therapist-approved. I'm not supposed to encourage you to eat your feelings, but you *might* weight 110 pounds soaking wet, have the metabolism of a cheetah, and this is your first real breakup. Exceptions can be made."

"Then bring on the binge. Ice cream first. I'll take the rocky road."

Allie blinked like she'd been expecting to share or maybe use bowls, but these were desperate times. "Okay. I'll take the mint chocolate chip. We're still using spoons, right?"

"Middle drawer to the right of the oven." Saralynn grabbed the quarts and dropped onto the sofa in her living room, setting Allie's ice cream on the coffee table while her sister retrieved utensils and the bag of marshmallows.

They ate in silence for a few minutes with the Home Shopping Network on mute, though Allie kept side-glancing. "You're really not gonna talk, huh?"

"I was getting around to it." Not really. She'd have gone the whole night without saying a word, relying on a sugar coma to usher her into an emotionless abyss. But that's not how Allie operated.

"Are you sure things are over between you two?"

Saralynn shrugged. "I haven't heard from him since he left. How much more over could they be?"

"Have you called or texted him?"

"Why would I do that?"

Allie stared for a solid ten seconds. "You're right. I can't think of a single reason. Oh, except to find out if you're still in a relationship?"

"Hey. Easy on the snarkasm. Brokenhearted bunny rabbit over here." She pointed to herself with the spoon and pulled out the quivering lower lip.

"Right. If bunny rabbits had piranha teeth and puma claws."

She let her mouth fall open and faked offense but didn't put a lot of effort into it. Allie was right. She normally had a pretty thick skin, and she'd gone to work every day like nothing was wrong. It was every minute outside of the arena when the teeth and claws morphed into tears and empty ice cream cartons.

"Okay, so I'm not helpless. But I am hurting, and that's not something I'd admit unless I had to. My eating habits have rapidly declined, and my metabolism won't last forever. I can't take the chance it'll go away before this awful feeling does. If it ever does. Does it?" Her voice went up at the end with a rush of anxiety.

"Okay, calm down. The awful feeling does go away eventually, but yours will hang around until you know for sure that it's time to move on. And you can't do that unless you talk to Madden."

"Is that really necessary? I don't want to be one of those clingy girls who can't take a hint. I mean, not a word in two weeks. I know what that means. I'm not gonna send a dozen texts he'll never answer or call when I know he won't pick up. That's pathetic." Her stomach sank, and her chest felt like there was a vise around it, squeezing tighter and tighter.

"Oh, bunny rabbit. We're in the process of ingesting three days' worth of calories in one night. We're like a half-block away from pathetic as it is. But seriously. You need to talk to him."

She leaned her head back against the couch and groaned. "Is talking your answer to everything?"

"You know I'm a therapist, right?" Allie opened the marshmallow bag and held it out.

Saralynn took a few and dropped them in her rocky road. "Fine. I'll call him tomorrow. What do I say?"

"Tell him you just want to see how he's doing. Ask what he's been up to. When he plans to come back to Vegas. Fair warning: men are not good with context clues. So then, I'm afraid, you'll have to ask what he wants for the two of you. If you want, I can come back and be here when you call."

The thought of flaying herself open and more or less begging for him to pour salt in her wounds was worth reconsidering the ostrich approach. *What I don't know can't hurt me.* Except it could. It was. And the only way to escape it was a direct confrontation. Why did Allie always have to be right? "That's okay. I need to do it on my own. No promises that I won't come over the minute I hang up, though."

"Our door is always open."

She took a big spoonful of chocolate courage. "You know, you're really good at this. People should pay you for it or something."

"People who aren't my baby sis-in-law?"

"Yeah, those people." Saralynn smiled and flipped channels until she landed on a romantic comedy. Maybe she'd crashed and burned in her first relationship test drive, but Jennifer Aniston seemed to have it all figured out. Tomorrow she'd face the smoking wreckage. Tonight she'd eat her weight in sugar and borrow some of Allie's bravery.

Chapter Thirty-Nine

Saturday, April 26th

It felt surreal pulling into the horseshoe drive. Two weeks seemed more like two years. Cleveland might as well be a separate planet. The weird part was, both places felt like home now. He parked and pulled out his phone, replaying the voicemail he'd heard twenty times in the past four days:

Mr. Vaughn, this is Ryan Keller. You had a very strong interview, and your credentials are impressive. We think you'd be a good fit at our firm. Call me back to finalize the details. Beep.

It would be a job. A normal job out of the media spotlight and scrutiny. Away from the tempting, neon pull of Vegas. Away from Saralynn. That thought stopped him just like it did every time he played the message. He hadn't talked to her since that last conversation in the elevator. Every time he'd picked up the phone and started to dial, his lack of answers stopped him. She would have had questions, hard ones, and he hadn't known what to say. He did now.

He owed her more than this. And the thought of leaving her for good kept him awake at night. But he needed to make a drastic change, and working at Keller's firm would accomplish that. He just couldn't get excited about a life without that frustrating, stubborn, beautiful, loyal woman in it.

Before he could get out of the car, Jacey pulled in behind him. Noon on the dot. Even pregnant and puking three hours a day, his sister was perfectly punctual. He hopped out and opened her door for her. "Hey, sis." Her forehead was clammy when he kissed it, and he tried not to make a face. "Thanks for meeting me."

"You said it was important."

"It is. How 'bout we get out of the sun?" He gestured toward the double front doors and walked with a hand on her back. Surprisingly, she didn't bat him away and insist she was pregnant not an invalid. Either she needed the proximity or knew that he did. The living room might have been more comfortable, but they'd always had their heart-to-hearts in the kitchen, so he led the way and pulled out a stool for her before sitting on the edge of one himself.

"Well, you already quit, and I know *you're* not pregnant. What's the big news?" She met his eyes and appeared calm, but there was the slightest waver in her voice that he heard only because he'd become so attuned to it.

"I got a job at an accounting firm in Cleveland."

The unshakable Jacquelyn Celia Phlynn, a woman with one of the best poker faces he'd ever seen, stared at him in absolute shock. Her eyes grew to the size of quarters, and she almost fell off the stool. "You what?"

"I'm not taking it."

She pressed a hand to her chest. "You couldn't have led with that? You want to give a pregnant woman a heart attack?"

"I was trying to build up to something, but you're right. I could have framed it better."

"You're not moving back to Cleveland, are you? Maddie, if this is about what I said before, that's not how I feel. I was overwhelmed by how much my life was changing. I was afraid that you were falling into your old habits, and I panicked. But I know the truth now, and I should have known it all along."

"It wasn't your fault. I understood where you were coming from. But that's not it. Honestly, I considered moving back, taking the job. At least I'm qualified for it."

"Accounting isn't the only thing you're qualified for. You gave up stock trading for something more exciting when you moved here. You can't tell me you get goose bumps at the idea of living in a cloud-covered city and working at a random, bland firm where every day will be the same. You say you want to find your own way. I can already guarantee you that's not it. Isn't there something you really *want* to do? Something that would make you look forward to getting out of bed in the morning?"

"Hey, slow down. I'm *not* moving. I thought about all that, and ... do you think it'd be crazy if I opened my own business?"

"I assume you don't mean the trampoline water park laser tag."

"I was twelve when I came up with that idea. I still maintain it could have legs if managed properly. But no. I now know better than to ask for your thoughts on Wet and Wild Frontier Bounce Town."

"Good. Because the liability alone—"

"Jace. I got it. You set me straight fifteen years ago with your dream-smashing graphs and pie charts. I'm serious. Would it be realistic to start a debt consulting business? It wouldn't just be that. I'd help people consolidate, set up budgets, offer day-to-day counseling, and help set them up for the future. And if gambling paid a part in their circumstances, who better to offer advice?"

The excited, confident expression on her face was a lot more encouraging than the patronizing one she'd given his preteen self. "Literally no one better. Maddie, I think that's a *great* idea. You have money for the start-up, and if you ever had to, you could always go back to straight accounting, but I don't think that'll be a problem."

The more he thought about it, the more he couldn't wait to get started. "And Vegas would be the best place for something like this."

"Absolutely. And not for nothing ... " She set a hand on her stomach. "Little Peanut here's going to need a fun uncle. Seeing as his mother lacks the gene."

How many times had he told her, "You're no fun"? Probably more than she deserved. Though teasing, her sentiment made him beam from the inside out. "Aw, you're fun. The kid'll need someone to show him how to check out books from the library."

She wrinkled her nose and kicked him in the shin just hard enough to sting. Then her gaze turned thoughtful. Uh-oh. Serious sisterly advice ahoy. "Have you talked to Saralynn? She asked about you."

The murky regret returned, but it was accompanied by a mirage of hope. "She did?"

"I guess that answers my question. Of course she did. You two were … well, I don't know what you were, but it obviously meant a lot to both of you. I know in the past I've stayed out of your relationships except for Linden, and that one was against my will. But I like Saralynn. I like her for you. I've seen her do everything in her power to fight for you and look out for you even at risk to herself. She's a good one."

"I know. She's why I can't leave." Over and over Saralynn had proven she deserved his trust and honestly cared. Even when he didn't earn it.

"You should tell her that."

Chapter Forty

Saturday Night

Apparently, heartsick felt the same as the flu. Saralynn pulled a blanket around her shoulders while shivering through a cold sweat. If this was love, maybe she'd had it right before. Keeping people at arm's length lowered the risk of anxiety-puking on your new Coach tennis shoes. She had to call him. She'd promised Allie. Pinkie swears aside, she had to know. If the only way to get past this horrible feeling and come out the other side was to trudge through it, then damn it, she'd trudge.

She wiped her palms on her jeans, tucked her legs up on the couch, and picked up her phone. She actually had to scroll through her call log. Not too long ago, he'd been right at the top. *No more wallowing thoughts.* Before she could come up with another reason to wait, she closed her eyes and pressed "Call."

It rang once. Twice. Then someone knocked on her door. She shrieked and jumped, and her phone flew halfway across the room. A slow breath steadied her nerves just enough to answer the door. Madden stood on the other side, Sinatra crooning in his hip pocket. He gave her a half-smile and pulled out his phone, swiping his thumb across the screen to silence Frank.

"Hi."

There was a response to that, right? There had to be. There was something simple she should say back, but her mind went totally blank. He looked incredible in the way that only he could. Designer denim that was most likely new but looked relaxed and lived-in. A faded T-shirt that hugged his torso. Clean-shaven with slightly rumpled strawberry blond hair that looked like he'd run his hands through it several times. His heady cologne almost pulled her closer with its tempting notes of ocean and citrus. Almost.

"Can I come in?"

She wanted to say no. She wanted to stay fuming and tell him off. But he was looking at her with those Madden eyes, so earnest and open. Ironically, it was when he turned off the charm that he was at his most charming. She still couldn't settle on a verbal response, but she stepped out of the way so he could get past her.

He stood just inside the living room, like he didn't feel entitled to go any farther, and she kind of agreed with that, but it hurt too much to hold the grudge. She resumed her spot on the sofa and gestured to the chair catty-corner to it.

Madden sat but leaned his forearms on his thighs, hands loosely folded. "I owe you a really big apology."

"For what?" *That's it. Play it cool.* She'd had a lot of practice. Except that was with guys she honestly hadn't cared about. Playing it cool then hadn't been a strategy, just a state of being. Not so easy now. *Okay, forget cool. Just don't cry.*

"What I *don't* owe you an apology for might be a shorter list. But for leaving like that. Not calling or texting. I left you hanging, and I'm sorry. That wasn't right or fair. I wanted to so many times, but I didn't know what to say. I pushed you away, and I didn't mean to do that."

It's okay wasn't a good reply because he'd just admitted that it wasn't okay. Still, she had to acknowledge the apology, so she bobbed her head. The subtle anxiety she'd been battling for two weeks started to subside, but it didn't vanish completely. He'd said he was sorry. He didn't say he still wanted to be with her. *Painful process. Happy ending.* Allie's words gave her the courage to finally say something. "I thought you might move back to Cleveland."

He nodded, and it felt like a hot knife in her chest.

She had no right to ask, but when had that ever stopped her? "Would it mean anything if I said I didn't want you to go?"

His eyes widened slightly, and he looked at her like he was seeing her for the first time. "No."

Her heart fell, and she turned away. She was about to break that oath not to cry when his hand closed around hers and tugged her back toward him.

"Saralynn. It would mean everything."

That was it. She cried away at least $50 of makeup, but she didn't care. Madden stood and pulled her into his arms, and she hiccupped against his chest.

He cradled her close and stroked her hair. "I'm so sorry. I did find a job in Cleveland, but I'm not going anywhere, okay?"

She wiped under her eyes even though it was useless and looked up at him. "You found a job? You're not staying here just because of me, are you?"

"I want to start a debt counseling business. Put all my mistakes to good use. There's no better place for that than Vegas. And I want to be close when Jace has the baby. Be a better uncle than the brother I've been. But those are just perks. When you find the one person who sees the real you and still wants to stick around, you do everything in your power to keep her. You're a damn good reason. You can't disagree."

"I love you." Her whole life, those words had stuck in her throat, but they tumbled out now, and the truth of them kept her from feeling anything but happy.

"I love you. And I will never leave you again." He held her face in his hands and leaned down for a soft kiss. Screw that. She wound her arms around his neck and bowed into him, kicking up the heat. He smiled against her lips and took the hint, picking her up so her legs wrapped around his waist. Without breaking the kiss, he carried her into the bedroom and lay back on the mattress, taking her with him. For the next hour, she took her time making sure he had absolutely no doubts that he'd made the right decision. He gave as well as he received, and any lingering embarrassment about breaking down earlier disappeared under his gentle touch and the way he looked at her like she was the only person in the universe.

Afterward, she curled up against him with her head on his chest, listening to his heartbeat. She traced a finger over the hard lines of his stomach.

"If you're thinking about round two, I'm gonna need a minute."

She grinned and laid her hand flat. "What are you thinking?"

"I'm thinking that, against all odds, the most amazing woman in the world gave me three chances. Best winning streak of my life."

"Yeah, well the sweetest man in the world chose me even though I self-destructed every previous relationship before they even started. I was a gamble."

"But look what I won."

"We both won." She held him closer, and he tightened his grip too. Two long shots who hit the jackpot.

Chapter Forty-One

Thursday, November 27th

"Madden, come on! We gotta go."

He rounded the corner just as Saralynn swooped by him with an aluminum pan full of shaved turkey. "I'm right behind you. Just had to finish up a budget plan for a client."

She rolled her eyes and kissed his cheek. "It's Thanksgiving, and your sister just had a baby. I think you can take a small break." And before he could debate that, she headed for the car.

Cole handed him a tower of Tupperware. "Here's all the sides plus plastic forks. Tell Jacey and Phlynn congrats for me." Four years with the Sinners, two of them as replacement captain, and the kid still called Carter by his last name even though he wasn't a player anymore.

"Will do. You still going over to Reese's house?"

"Yeah, man. He said they made a big feast, so you know I'm there."

"Tell them we'll be by later. My sister might be Wonder Woman, but I bet even she will need some sleep after this morning."

"You got it." Cole slapped him on the back and pushed him toward the door.

The drive to the hospital was a blur, so it was a good thing Saralynn was at the wheel. All he could think about was meeting his nephew. He was an *uncle*. Surreal. They stopped at three nurses stations before finding the maternity ward.

Saralynn stepped up to the desk. "Hi. We're looking for Jacquelyn Vaughn. She delivered this morning."

The nurse with a name tag that said Zelda glanced down then back up. "Relation?"

Saralynn tilted her head toward Madden. "Brother. I'm a friend."

"Well her husband is already with her, and we normally only allow two visitors at a time, but it is a holiday, and I can see you brought sustenance. Room 204." Zelda winked.

"*Thank* you. There's plenty of food here. You're welcome to stop in and make a plate. Happy Thanksgiving." Saralynn flashed her get-out-of-jail-free smile and headed down the hall.

"Same, dears."

Madden nodded to Zelda then trailed after the woman who added much-needed order and structure to his life. She kept him going in every possible way, and after only nine short months, he couldn't imagine being without her.

When he walked into Jacey's room, he almost dropped the Tupperware. She sat propped up on pillows, happier than he'd ever seen her, staring at the bundle in her arms. She looked up at him and glowed. "Hey. Come meet your nephew. Jonathan Mario Phlynn."

He laughed and set the food on a corner chair then stood over the bed. "Sis, I was kidding about the video game suggestions."

Carter, who stood on the opposite side, shook his head. "Mario the hockey player, not the plumber."

"Ahhh. Makes more sense. And Jonathan for Dad?"

"And you." Jacey smiled. "Your middle name, Madden Jonathan."

His heart swelled until it almost couldn't fit inside his chest. *Hold it together.* Saralynn took the spot by his side and set a hand on his back, like she knew he needed it in that moment.

"Can I hold him?"

"Sure, Uncle Maddie." Jacey very carefully lifted the baby. Carter even held his hands out just in case, but Madden had it covered.

"You will *not* encourage that nickname." He kept his voice soft and couldn't maintain a serious tone. She definitely would encourage it. He might as well accept that now. As he rocked his nephew side to side, Saralynn swayed with him, her head on his shoulder, and he knew. He was all in.

More from This Author
(From *Full Strength* by Katie Kenyhercz)

Tuesday, April 16th

Allie released a deep breath and straightened the framed degrees on the wall. Silence settled so thick, she could almost hear her heartbeat. It was hard to tell if it was a blessing or a curse being sequestered in the basement. On one hand, players would have one less excuse to avoid her because she was right next to the locker room. On the other hand, having no windows felt a little like being buried alive. The few landscape paintings at least gave the illusion of nature and made it more bearable.

A light knock on her office door made her tense, but she forced her shoulders down before she turned around to face her guest. Her heart beat double time, but it slowed when her boss stepped inside instead of her first patient.

Jacey Phlynn, owner of the Las Vegas Sinners, looked put together as usual in a black skirt suit and emerald silk blouse. As Jacey closed the door, Allie caught a glimpse of her red-soled pumps. Louboutin. She felt self-conscious in her JC Penney knockoffs, but three degrees didn't come cheap.

"Allie, I'm glad I caught you early. I know you're good on Reese's history, but I wanted to give you a heads-up—"

"He doesn't want to do this."

Jacey's eyes widened, her mouth fell open, and she shook her head.

Allie could see her boss scrambling for a polite denial, and she laughed. "It's okay. I would have rather peeled my skin off with a cheese grater than see my first shrink after my injury."

"That's right. I'm sorry. I'm sure you know exactly what to say. I wish I did."

"Let me guess. He paid you a visit; tried to get out of it."

Jacey sighed, pressed her lips together.

"It's all right. He needs this whether he knows it or not."

"I just—he may say things. Seem uncooperative. He hasn't been himself since it happened. He's a great goalie and a huge asset to this team, but if he can't get past this, we might have to trade him, and I don't want to do that. He's surgically attached to my husband. We're talking shared organs. If separated, one or both might not survive. But now that Carter's involved with the business side of the team, he has to see things as a GM would— even if that means trading his best friend. If there's any way to avoid that, I have to try."

Allie smiled as she remembered press pictures of Shane Reese with his best friend and ex-captain, Carter Phlynn. The two had played together their entire careers. Phlynn's had ended just last season with a concussion. Hard to believe *he* didn't need some therapy, too. "Reese's recovery will depend on him, but I'll do everything I can to get him there."

"Bless you. We are ... *I* am so glad to have you here. Thank you again for starting on such short notice."

"I'm happy to be here. I'm excited to work with this team."

Jacey's barely suppressed laughter wasn't reassuring. Especially when she followed it up with, "Hold that thought."

• • •

"Hey, Reese. You ready to talk about your feelings?"

"Shut up." Shane Reese ignored Kevin Scott, his teammate and tormentor. Instead, he stared at the cement block wall while his friends dressed for practice. The twentieth practice he'd miss.

"Leave him alone, Scotty. Bad enough as it is."

"Thanks, Cole. Big help." Shane glanced at the hotshot rookie, Dylan Cole, who earned captaincy in his second NHL season and tried to rein in his anger. That's what got him into this mess in the first place. Cole gave him the innocent act and held up his hands. Nine years younger, and the kid thought he was Yoda or something.

Reese rolled his eyes and pushed off the bench. "Whatever. Guess I should get it over with."

"Hey, before you go ... got you these." Scott turned from his locker and tossed him a box of tissues. Reese ground his teeth and threw the box back. Hard. It hit Scott between the shoulders but bounced off, harmless. The asshole was laughing.

"All right, that's enough," Cole broke in. "Scotty, hit the ice before Coach sees you missing. If you're the last out again, she'll give you a speech that'll make your ears bleed. And mine, so spare me. Reese, go talk to the doc. It won't be that bad."

"That's why you're captain, Cole. Your speeches are so damn inspiring." And before he could get another one, Reese stormed from the locker room. It would have been more dramatic without the limp, and that made him angrier. High ankle sprain. It was such a stupid injury. If that ass Chekov hadn't landed on him like that, he wouldn't be indefinitely benched at the start of the playoffs.

He had to consciously unclench his fists as he stopped at the dark wood door with the newly minted plaque. Dr. Alexandra Kallen, Sports Psychologist. He could just imagine what she looked like. Gray hair in a tight bun. Librarian glasses. Judging smirk and zero idea of what he was going through. He summoned some resolve and knocked.

"It's open."

The voice didn't *sound* old. He stepped inside, and could only stare. Alexandra Kallen was no librarian. A fitted, short sleeve, red blouse played off the coloring of dark brown hair that fell in straight layers a few inches past her shoulders. She looked more co-ed than doctor in her leg-hugging, dark denim pants and high heels that put her even with his chin. When he took her extended hand, her skin felt soft, but her grip firm. "You don't look old enough to be a doctor."

"Thank you, but I'm twenty-eight."

"Sure you don't mean eighteen?"

She arched a brow. "You're one to talk. You have your driver's license yet?"

"You don't sound like a doctor either."

She laughed, and when her features relaxed, she looked even younger. "Thanks, I think. You're Shane Reese? It's nice to meet you."

"I, uh, you too. Um, what should I call you? Dr. Kallen?"

Her full smile showed perfectly shaped, white teeth. No lipstick, just gloss. It didn't look like she wore any other makeup, but she was a striking, girl-next-door kind of pretty. "If you want. Or you can call me Allie. Whatever you're comfortable with."

Allie. That fit much better than Dr. Kallen. "Oh—kay."

She pressed her lips together and looked down at their still-joined hands.

"Sorry." He let go and looked around the room. Anywhere but at her. At least until the heat faded from his cheeks. Her office wasn't what he expected either. He thought it would be something like Jacey's—modern, minimalistic. Instead, it looked like the family room from his childhood home; pale blue paint disguising the cement-block walls, overstuffed furniture, plush cream carpet. A mini fridge sat next to the couch, and a bowl of pumpkin seeds beckoned from the coffee table. "How'd you know?"

"The pumpkin seeds? I asked around. Have a seat." She gestured toward the couch and sat in the chair adjacent to it.

Reese hesitated but lowered himself onto the sofa. He didn't know what to think of her talking to others behind his back. It seemed ... manipulative. "You gonna tell me you know the name of my first dog, too?"

"Does it bother you that I did some research?"

"This whole thing bothers me."

"I know what you mean." Her voice was smooth and quiet, and it gnawed on his nerves.

"All due respect, Doc, but I seriously doubt—"

"Junior year."

"What?"

"Junior year." She turned her dark gaze on him, but her voice remained soft, her expression unreadable. "I played netminder for Stanford University's soccer team. Number one in the division. My junior year, I tore my ACL blocking a shot, and I never played on a team again."

"If that's your idea of a pep talk …"

She laughed again. A sweet, genuine sound that warmed him even though he wanted to be mad. She leaned back and crossed her legs. "No. I'm just saying I know what it's like when an injury takes away the one thing you care about the most. It's why I went into sports psychology. Helping other athletes helped me." Her gaze darted to the side then down to her notes. Interesting. Doc might have more secrets than she was owning up to.

She cleared her throat. "And your injury is different. It may take a while, but it'll heal. You'll get back out there."

"Yeah … even if I do, now it'll be prone to re-injury. It'll follow me for the rest of my career."

"It may; it may not. Lots of players get a high ankle sprain, take a few months off, and come back better than before. Not all of them re-injure it. And you're not going to let this stop you from having a career. Right?"

"This is the *playoffs*. We have a real chance this year. I worked my ass off all season, and now I don't get to play?"

She fell quiet. He'd heard about this trick. If she didn't talk, he'd have to fill the silence. Fat chance. But she didn't *stay* quiet.

"Do you know why you're here?"

He tilted his head back to count ceiling tiles. "Boss thinks you'll help me 'cope' with warming the bench."

"Actually, it's because you fought two of your teammates and put your fist through the physical therapy wall."

He groaned and slid his hands over his face. "I apologized for that. I paid for the wall. And I shouldn't have engaged with them, but they wouldn't let up, and I couldn't take it anymore. So, what, this is anger management?"

"In a way. I want to help you deal with the frustration so you don't damage any more property … or people. Injury is part of the game. Even for goalies. I know it's not easy to accept that."

And she did know. He wanted to hold onto the idea that no one could understand, but from what she said, she knew exactly how he felt. It kind of pissed him off.

Maybe I do *need to be here.*

The rational part of his brain—the part missing since his last minutes on the ice—reminded him he shouldn't blame this woman. It wouldn't kill him to be nice to her. If things were different, if she weren't trying to autopsy his subconscious, he'd probably ask her out. As it was, it took every ounce of his self-control to stay in the room. But he had to stick with the program. "Whatever you say, Doc."

• • •

Allie watched him and made sure to keep her expression neutral. She'd seen him in pictures before, but in person he was a lot … bigger. Not the tallest on the team, but a good half-foot taller than her five feet, six inches. And solid. They called him The Wall, and she could see why with the way he filled out a designer t-shirt and jeans. In all of his press pictures, he smiled wide, and the gleam in his whiskey brown eyes reflected his league-renowned playful personality. Not now. Now his eyes were blank, but his white-knuckled grip on the armrest said anger simmered under the surface.

Maybe he thought he was fooling her, or maybe he didn't care one way or the other. But she knew that fake complacent look. She'd worn it day in and day out for a year after her injury. Her chest felt tight. Professional distance was sometimes easier said than done. "Do you think you need to be here?"

He stared at the wall, lifted a shoulder.

Well, that was a big, fat no. "Shane—"

"Reese. Everybody calls me Reese. Even my parents."

"Reese. It's all right if you're angry. I'd be more concerned if you weren't. But it's important to work through it so you don't climb out of your skin while your ankle heals."

"Little late for that, or I wouldn't be here, right?"

Ah, there it was—some shame in his voice and a touch of humility. A good place to start. "Punching the wall was a moment of frustration. Everyone has them. And I'm willing to bet Collier and Scott weren't innocent angels supporting you from the sidelines."

He smirked.

"Right. I'm not condoning what you did to them; I'm just saying I know you were provoked."

"I was. But that's no excuse."

The last part sounded robotic, like a quote from his coach, Nealy Windham—something he'd had to write on a mental chalkboard a hundred times. It had her fabled corporal punishment ring to it. "You have a right to feel whatever you're feeling. Then, now, always. Just channel your reaction. You feel like taking down a teammate, hit the heavy bag instead."

He nodded. He may have heard it before, but he needed to keep hearing it until it sunk in. Still, that sheen of anger in his eyes remained. He wasn't just having a hard time sitting out. There was something else.

His pocket buzzed. He fished out a cell phone and hit a button. "Sorry. I have physical therapy at ten."

"It's all right. I think we're done for today anyway."

"Today …?"

"You didn't think this was a one-shot deal, did you?"

The look of abject shock said he did. Allie bit back a smile. "Sorry. You're stuck with me until you're back on the ice. Tuesdays and Thursdays."

His jaw tightened, and his fingers twitched before he stood. "I guess I'll see you Thursday then."

"See you Thursday."

Allie took in the tense set of his shoulders as he left, and she held her breath. Five seconds later, the crack of a hand slapping cinderblock echoed through the hall. At least the basement walls weren't plaster. She leaned back in the armchair and studied the ceiling. Shane Reese did not hide his feelings well, but that was good news. There might be hope for him yet.

In the mood for more Crimson Romance?
Check out *High Octane: Unleashed* by Ashlinn Craven at
CrimsonRomance.com.